Hoofbeats

Silence and Lily, 1773

by KATHLEEN DUEY

PUFFIN BOOKS

PUFFIN BOOKS
Published by the Penguin Group
Penguin Young Readers Group,
345 Hudson Street, New York, New York 10014, U.S.A.
Penguin Group (Canada), 90 Eglinton Avenue East, Suite 700, Toronto, Ontario,
Canada M4P 2Y3 (a division of Pearson Penguin Canada Inc.)
Penguin Books Ltd, 80 Strand, London WC2R 0RL, England
Penguin Ireland, 25 St Stephen's Green, Dublin 2, Ireland
(a division of Penguin Books Ltd)
Penguin Group (Australia), 250 Camberwell Road, Camberwell, Victoria 3124,
Australia (a division of Pearson Australia Group Pty Ltd)
Penguin Books India Pvt Ltd, 11 Community Centre, Panchsheel Park,
New Delhi - 110 017, India
Penguin Group (NZ), 67 Apollo Drive, Rosedale, North Shore 0745, Auckland,
New Zealand (a division of Pearson New Zealand Ltd.)
Penguin Books (South Africa) (Pty) Ltd, 24 Sturdee Avenue, Rosebank,
Johannesburg 2196, South Africa

Registered Offices: Penguin Books Ltd, 80 Strand, London WC2R 0RL, England

Published simultaneously in the United States of America
by Dutton Children's Books and Puffin Books,
divisions of Penguin Young Readers Group, 2007

1 3 5 7 9 10 8 6 4 2

CIP DATA IS AVAILABLE.

Puffin ISBN: 978-0-14-240909-1

Printed in the United States of America

For Diane, Linda, Sharon, and Dory. Thanks for galloping the canal road with me, for exploring every path along Little Dry Creek, out Longs Road past the siphon and on up into the foothills. Thanks for your friendship. A childhood set to the sound of hoofbeats—we were so lucky.

CHAPTER ONE

*W*e were all three sitting straight-backed, perched on the edges of our chairs with our feet tucked back, ankles crossed. Mrs. Chester was standing off to one side, watching us pretend to sip daintily from our empty cups. I could see Lily out the steamy, narrow window. She was tethered to the hitching rail, standing quietly, waiting for me.

"Heads high," Mrs. Chester said, and we all leveled our chins. She walked behind us, correcting our posture with gentle nudges. We had begun the day's instruction by reading the poetry of Phyllis Wheatley, the slave girl who had become so well known in the Massachusetts settlements. I loved speaking her words, learning to lift my voice, then let it fall. It was like singing the words, almost.

While raging tempests shake the shore,
While Ælus' thunders round us roar,
And sweep impetuous o'er the plain
Be still, O tyrant of the main . . .

But that part of the lesson was done. Now we were practicing tea manners. Yes, *tea* manners. These are different from ballroom manners, in some telling, but truly dull, ways. Sitting to my right, Anne looked bored. She had as little interest in this kind of instruction as I did. Sarah was paying close attention, as always—if any of us ended up marrying someone truly important, it would be her.

I glanced past Sarah and out the window again. I could see Lily shaking her mane. I sighed. I would much rather be riding my mare than learning manners, or even reciting fine poetry. Lily suddenly raised her head as though she had heard and understood my thought.

"Drop your shoulders, Miss Silence," Mrs. Chester said. "You look as broad as a boy squaring them like that."

I did as I was told, and she nodded. Then she went on to correct Anne's and Sarah's postures once more. Anne and Sarah. I envied my friends' names. My own was the result of my mother's carrying on the old-fashioned Puritan naming traditions. Silence had been her grandmother's godmother's name. I wished she hadn't given it to me, but she had.

I realized abruptly that Mrs. Chester was looking at me. I held my cup properly, wrist curved slightly, and sat with my spine straight, my shoulders down. And the instant she turned her gaze, I glanced out the window again. Our two hours had to be almost over. It wouldn't be long before Samuel and Elijah came to escort me home.

The weather had unexpectedly warmed enough so that Mother had let me ride Lily to my usual tutoring session—with my brother and our stable boy as escorts, of course. It had been wonderful, much nicer than jouncing along in the carriage bundled up to my ears in coach robes and blankets. I saw Lily shake her mane again. She was as restless as I was.

Mrs. Chester started a mock social conversation, asking after Anne's harpsichord lessons. Anne forgot herself and let her true passion for playing show as she answered. Mrs. Chester reminded us not to lean forward in social conversation in a vulgar, eager way. We all sat back a little, and Anne flattened her voice, modulating the tone demurely as she answered with less-obvious enthusiasm. Mrs. Chester nodded approval, then turned to one side and discreetly adjusted her wig.

I took the opportunity to look outside again. I was quick and careful and Mrs. Chester didn't notice. But Anne did, of course, and she made a face. Sarah shot me a wide-eyed, silly look. Then I saw Anne duck her chin and I knew she was trying not to giggle. Which made me cross my eyes at her, but then I had to bite my lower lip to keep myself from laughing.

I forced myself to stare blandly at Mrs. Chester as she turned back and told us, yet again—no doubt because she had caught a sidelong glimpse of us making faces—that young women who were too empty-headed to learn proper manners would end up in marriages with men of less-than-superior quality. She paused, looking from Anne's face to mine, then on to Sarah's. "A girl whose family cannot afford to educate her is no worse off than a girl who will not learn," she said, and we all sat up a little straighter again.

But I knew she was only partly right. My father was wealthy and as respected as any businessman in Boston. My mother had come from a farm family in England. She had met my father there, married him, then they had come to the colonies together. She had learned how to entertain guests, how to dance properly, how to play the harpsichord a little, and all the rest—*after* her marriage. I knew she was unusual, though. All my father's friends—including Anne's and Sarah's fathers—had married properly educated women from well-known Boston families.

"And how is your musical instruction progressing, Silence?" Mrs. Chester asked me. I answered carefully, keeping my voice soft and my diction clear. When I finished, she looked past me and arched her eyebrows. "There's your brother, Silence. Our time is nearly up, ladies. Let us say our good-byes."

Mrs. Chester had firm rules about leave-taking courtesies. We always said our farewells properly, politely. This week Anne was playing hostess, so Sarah and I had to thank her for at least two specific things we had enjoyed during our visit—without seeming to assume we would be invited again—before we took our leave. Then Mrs. Chester left the room.

"I saw William Dest at my cousin's wedding," Anne whispered the instant she was gone. Sarah and I leaned closer. Handsome William had all the older girls giggling. "He was talking to Maggie Halp most the evening," Sarah added. We all sighed. Maggie was seventeen and such a beauty. All the young men noticed her. I wondered what it felt like, having a boy making excuses just to talk a bit. *Flirting.*

We said our real good-byes, and I went to get my heavy woolen cape from the coat tree by the door. Once it was tied it around my shoulders, I nearly ran out the door. Lily whinnied at me as I hurried toward her. Samuel laughed as he got down to give me a boost into my sidesaddle. I straightened my skirts and smiled at Elijah as Sam turned the stirrup for me. Elijah's nose was pink—it was a little colder than it had been two hours before.

We clip-clopped down the street, then, instead of heading home, Samuel led us along Mill Pond Road and through the woods on the far end. We talked about everything and nothing, both of them teasing me when I described the day's lessons with Mrs. Chester. By the time we circled back into town, I felt wonderful. What a grand day. I had seen my two best friends, and I had gotten to ride Lily—and I had escaped nearly half a day of housework with my mother.

We started back down Hannover—turning onto Tremont Street, then onto Beacon, to get to the wide-open expanse of the Common. Lily tossed her head and pulled at the reins as we came onto the yellowing grass.

This stretch of land had been set aside for grazing cows and horses long ago. Now, people used it for much more than that. The school was nearby, and sometimes the children were brought here to run and fly kites or play games. In the summertime, men trained hunting dogs here. In the winter, if the fresh snow wasn't melted by cold rains, the boys staged snowball fights, dodging around the trees. But today, there was no snow except in patches under the trees, and the grassy field was almost empty. I saw two men walking on the far end, where the marsh formed the edge of the Common—no one else. Lily tossed her head again. I reached down to pat her neck, and she sidled.

"Lily wants to race," Samuel called. "Shall we, Silence?" I didn't answer, so he tried again, louder. "Silence? Will you race?"

I turned to look at my brother. His gelding was prancing, switching its tail. I glanced at Elijah. He was grinning at Sam. Were they planning a trick? My whole life they had delighted in playing jokes on me. More than once, people had assumed Elijah was my brother because of the way he and Samuel acted, helping each other with whatever task was at hand, laughing at each other's jokes.

Elijah was on one of Father's best mares, and she was fidgeting, too. All three horses were ready for a good gallop—and they all knew the Common was the place for it. I would race, of course. Still, I hesitated. I wanted to see what stakes Samuel would set on it. He always thought of something good, something I couldn't resist.

"Silence?" he shouted after a long moment. "The one who loses has to explain to Mother why we are late getting back."

I heard Elijah laugh, and I stuck my tongue out at him. He wouldn't be explaining anything to anyone. Mother would assume Samuel or I was responsible. She would be right, as usual. It had been so lovely to ride along the Mill Pond, to talk about next year's foals, the weather, Mother's cherished pumpkins having been even bigger than usual this year, about nothing at all. It was wonderful to just feel *happy*. At home, in the merchant shops, in all of Boston, there was a constant hum of worry now—worse than usual, worse than ever before.

The newest uproar was because King George was levying more new taxes—on tea this time—and my father and all his friends were worried about it. The king had made the East India Company the only tea merchant to serve the colonies, and now he was demanding that the people pay a tax on the tea. Everyone was furious. There were three ships in the harbor that hadn't been unloaded—the captains were afraid to try to dock at all, afraid that the crowds of angry men might start fights. Samuel said that the talk in the taverns was getting harsher. Men were beginning to talk about refusing the king's orders altogether, about outright rebellion.

War.

The idea terrified me.

"Afraid your skinny little mare can't win?" Samuel teased, and I was grateful to be pulled back out of my uneasy thoughts. I heard Elijah stifle another laugh. He loved it when Lily and I beat Samuel and his long legged gelding—and we often did. Elijah said something to Samuel that I couldn't hear, and they both shook their heads, then looked at me with mock pity on their faces. That did it.

"Our usual course?"

"Yes," Samuel answered, and Elijah echoed it.

"Then count it off, Samuel!" I shouted, pretending to be irritated. I wasn't. I was excited. I loved galloping Lily.

Elijah quickly reined my father's mare to one side to give us all room for an even start. We spread out, Elijah and I glancing at Samuel.

"One, two, three, go!" Samuel shouted, and we all three cheated, as we always did, urging our horses into a gallop on the two-count. I leaned over Lily's neck as she sprang forward, letting her out, my left foot steady in the single stirrup, my weight forward on my sidesaddle. I moved with her stride. I knew Lily's gaits perfectly, her rhythm, the way she flattened out when she was serious about galloping hard. And she was serious this morning, as usual.

As Lily settled into a gallop, I moved with her, pushing off the stirrup a little harder to keep my weight forward as she hit her long, reaching stride. Samuel's gelding pounded along beside us as I began the long curve toward the hill where the watch house stood. We all three galloped around it once, far side first, then reined hard to head toward the marshes on the west side of the Common.

Lily had gained a lead by the time we got there, and we all reined in to go around the tree stump we used as a marker on this end of our racecourse. From there it was a long straightaway back to the lane set off by maple trees. I got there first and made the sharp turn fairly well, reining in just enough to be sure Lily could make it, then I loosened the reins again as we galloped between the trees all the way back to the granary. Lily and I were a little wide on the last turn, but it didn't matter. Samuel and his gelding were a good three or four strides behind us, and Elijah was another stride back from Samuel.

On the last leg of the course, Samuel's gelding gained ground on us. I urged Lily faster, leaning so low over her neck that her mane brushed my cheeks as we flew over the ground, crossing the Common one last time, then clattering up Frog Lane, past the Talbots' place, then the granges, then the pastures that surround my father's house.

Once I was in sight of our barn—and nearing the tall fence post we used as a finish line—I glanced back again. Samuel was just two strides behind us now, and Elijah was less than half a length behind him—but we had won!

As the post flashed past, I sat upright and pulled Lily in steadily, getting her back into a canter, then down to a spanking trot as we all turned into the carriage yard behind the barn. "Ahhhch!" Samuel shouted, laughing.

I reached down to rub Lily's neck as I reined in again, bringing her to a walk, telling her what a grand mare she was, how fast, how strong. The course we had devised was over a mile long, and she was breathing quick and deep as we all rode a slow, wide circle to let the horses catch their breath. Samuel made some excuse about a bird flushed from the marsh grass startling his gelding into shying, but he was smiling as he said it, so I knew he was joking. My brother loves me enough to really try to win, so that when I do beat him at anything, I know I can be proud.

Elijah looked happy as he dismounted, then helped me down. I knew he could not take the chances Samuel or I did as we raced—my father would never forgive him for injuring a horse, or himself. And he wouldn't dare win over Samuel, anyway, for fear my father would think he had forgotten his place.

Father had bought Elijah's indenture when he had been just four years old, right after he had been orphaned. Now, at fourteen, Elijah was as good with horses as any grown man—but he still had six years to complete his contract with my father.

Samuel and I handed Elijah our reins, and I watched as he led all three horses back down the lane. He always walked them cool before he rubbed them down and put them back in their stalls. He stopped abruptly and turned back to shout at Samuel. "The gelding is favoring his left front!" I heard Samuel catch his breath as Elijah bent and ran his hands over the gelding's leg, tracing the tendons, grasping his pastern, waiting for the gelding to wince. He didn't. Elijah lifted his hoof. Then he straightened. "It's a stone bruise. Rest should heal it." I heard Samuel exhale in relief. A stone bruise took time to heal, but it *would* heal. It was much less serious than a leg injury would have been.

We turned and walked toward the house. Old Simon was standing at the wide double doors of the barn, and he grinned at me, shaking his head and wagging his index finger. I knew why, because he had told me more than once. He always said I was the exact opposite of my mother as a girl—she had loved having tea parties with her dolls. Simon had known my mother all her life. He had belonged to her family all of his sixty years.

Samuel tousled my hair as we walked and I ducked, smiling, even though it bothered me a little. I was twelve now, not five or six.

"Silence!" I heard my mother call. "Samuel? Come in quickly, please." I glanced at my brother, and he nodded, running a few steps ahead to keep his loser's pledge. I walked a little quicker, curious to know what he would say.

My brother rarely fibs. He is just adept at telling the truth in a way that makes people understand. If I had been the one to explain the wonderful chill in the air, the horses prancing sideways and all the rest, my mother would not have been charmed. But the way Samuel made it sound, I saw her eyes light—probably remembering some crisp, happy day from her own farm-girl childhood.

Even now that she lived on the very edge of Boston, with its markets and wagonloads of farm goods, Mother still kept a big garden, rarely needing to buy anything for our table. And she had talked my father into buying a farm sixty miles to the south with apple trees and a wide creek. He had leased it to a Quaker family, but one day, I knew, my mother wanted to live there, at least in the summers.

"Your father is in the parlor with friends," she told Samuel when he was finished. "He wants you to join them." Then she turned to face me as Samuel went down the hall.

"I told you last night that I would be busy washing the floors upstairs and that Prissy would need your help in the kitchen this morning."

I exhaled. She had. And I had forgotten completely when Samuel woke me. We had left early, to have more time to dawdle on the way to Mrs. Chester's lessons. "I'm sorry," I said, knowing it wouldn't be enough.

"You should have asked me if you could leave so early."

I nodded. "I just forgot and—"

"You forget everything but that horse," she said.

I started to apologize once more, but she held up one hand to stop me. "It isn't just this once, Silence," she said. "You forgot to help Prissy in the root cellar day before yesterday, too. She had to turn fifty pumpkins herself and then go through the apple barrels."

"I will apologize to her. I know she won't mind and—"

"Really?" my mother said sharply. "What do you expect her to say? Your father owns her. Would she allow herself to be angry at his daughter?"

"Prissy would tell me if she minded, and I would—"

"Silence!" my mother cut me off.

I stared at the floor planks. I cannot abide it when she makes a command out of my name.

Silence. I hate it. Why not name me Timidity or Little Miss MeekandMild? My mother's name is Charity, and she got it the same way I got Silence. Her family is so old-fashioned.

My mother had told me, all my life, about the farm chores she had done as a girl. The work she had done made mine look small and simple, of course. But the truth was this: Very few of my friends had to work in the house the way I did. Their servants did everything—and so they had more time for doing their needlework and practicing with their music tutors and learning the cut paper art of Madame Demming and—

"Prissy will be in the washhouse tomorrow, and I will need your help inside. I think it best that you don't ride for a while," my mother said. "Simon can take you to Mrs. Chester's weekly sessions in the carriage."

I blinked, snatched out of my thoughts. Then I exhaled, wishing she had chosen any punishment but that one. But, of course, she had chosen what she knew would matter most to me. I knew better than to argue with her, or to try to make her say how long *a while* would be. Any lack of manners on my part and she would lengthen the time.

Dragging my feet, feeling almost sick, I went down the hall to change out of my riding frock so I could begin my afternoon chores. But once I was in my room and my door was closed, I cried. Not just for myself, even though I loved riding Lily more than anything else. I cried for my sweet mare. By forbidding me to ride, my mother would be punishing Lily. She was the one who would be cooped up in her stall, restless and uneasy—and not understanding why I was neglecting her.

CHAPTER TWO

❧ ❧ ❧

*I*t turned colder. There was no new snow, but the wind was fierce early in the morning, rattling the shutters. I almost envied Prissy, out in the washhouse, with the boiling pots and the warm steam rising from the hot soapy water. She would be doing heavy work until nightfall, but she would be warm.

My father spent nearly all day in the parlor, talking in hushed voices with three men I didn't know, and two that I did: Anne's father was there, and Sarah's. I knew what they were doing, more or less, because Samuel had told me. They were reading and discussing the broadsides that had been posted, arguing about the tea, about what might be done about asking the king to reconsider the tax, about the growing anger in Boston.

That's a secret Samuel and I share. He taught me to read when I was six. Really read, I mean, not just the few words my tutor taught me. Samuel knew he was not supposed to, but I talked him into it. I wanted to do everything he did back then. I would have followed him off the edge of a cliff, I think. Now that I am twelve, I still love him, but it has changed. I don't think he is perfect anymore—just wonderful.

Mother taught me to read receipts when I was ten. She thought I was uncommon quick in learning, but she never suspected I already knew how. It is important to her that I become a skilled housewife, that I am able to keep accounts and write down receipts of dishes my husband likes. But she would be furious with Samuel if she knew that I could read almost anything. I don't know what she—or my father— would think if they knew I sometimes read the *Boston News-Letter* and the broadsides Father leaves in the parlor.

Samuel is learning Latin and Greek now, and the principals of mathematics. He will go to Harvard College when he finishes with his tutors. I envy him all the books they have there. I envy his invitations into Father's parlor meetings, too.

Every time I had to pass the parlor door doing my chores that day, I walked slowly, hoping to hear something through the thick maplewood planks. I heard what sounded like shouting once, but I could not understand what was being said.

The angry voices made me wonder. Raking the ashes out of my parents' bedroom hearth, I found myself thinking that maybe some of my father's friends—all loyal to England and the king, of course—were beginning to disagree among themselves about the king's new taxes.

Carrying a stack of clean linens back up the hall near sunset—knowing the men would all leave soon to avoid riding in the dark—I paused for an instant and pressed my ear against the parlor door.

My mother saw me. Before I could even try to pretend that I was looking at the tall clock that stands near the door, she was beside me, grasping my hand and yanking me back down the hall. She pulled me into the kitchen.

"Eavesdropping!" she whispered. When my mother is truly upset with me, her mouth has a way of tightening so that her words can barely squeeze through her teeth. I stared at the flames in the hearth, hoping she would not lengthen the *while* I would not be allowed to ride—but dreading that she would.

My heart aching, furious with myself, I looked at my mother. "May I please scrub floors, or I could do wash instead of Prissy? Or carry out the chamber pots? Or—"

My mother held up one hand to quiet me. "A child of three is charming when she leans against a closed door to hear her father's voice. You are twelve, and you know that doors are closed for good reason. And a girl has no business in men's affairs."

I took in a breath to argue, and she said my name like a cat hissing. "Silence! Go to your bedchamber."

I walked down the hall, jerked at the iron latch, and opened my door. I knew better than to close it hard enough for my mother to hear. I eased it shut behind me then perched on the edge of my bed, staring at the floor, shifting, trying to find a comfortable position. My bedstraw was matted and getting harder by the night—and the ropes creaked. It was time to empty out the ticking mattress, get rid of the flattened straw and put in fresh—and tighten and wax the ropes. I had been putting off asking Mother if I could have a new bed—one big enough so that I could straighten my legs entirely. She loved to get every half penny's worth out of whatever we used, but I had grown fast in the past year. This was not the day to ask for anything, though, that much was certain.

I smoothed my skirt and sat up straight for a long time, wanting to be prim and ladylike when Mother came and opened the door to tell me my punishment—or to let me apologize and be done with it. But time dragged past, and I finally slouched back against the wall, swinging my legs, my skirts up above my knees. And of course, it was in that instant that the door latch lifted. I wrenched upright, stiff and blushing as the door opened just enough to admit my brother's voice. "Silence?"

"Samuel?" I said back to him.

"Siiiilenssssse?" he said in a voice like a villain in a story.

"Samuelllllllllllll!" I answered, in the high, quavering voice of a desperate heroine.

He laughed and swung open the door. "Mother sent me to tell you that you may come help, then stay to supper." He made a face. "She didn't say what you did to offend her this time, but I warn you, supper is peas porridge again. It might not be worth your trouble getting back into her good graces."

Samuel whispered that last part. He is tall now, almost sixteen, and he pretends that he isn't afraid of anything. But he is still fearful of displeasing Mother. So am I. So are all the servants and the stable boys and even my father, at least sometimes. She is small, with the hands and feet of a child, and rosy cheeks, but she is ferocious once she sets her mind to a thing. She bought a two-stone sack of dried peas from a farmer at the Faneuil Market because they had been uncommon cheap. We would be eating them until springtime.

"Thinking about months of peas porridge?" Sam asked. Sometimes he can guess my thoughts. I nodded.

"There is to be a roast chicken this night, to go with it." He smiled, and made a clucking sound, which made me laugh again.

"Are the men arguing?" I asked in a low voice.

He nodded solemnly. "There were some strong opinions today. Father was disturbed by a lot of what was said." I waited for him to say more, but he didn't. I followed him back up the hall. The parlor door was still closed. He continued toward it when I stopped at the kitchen. I watched him knock. A voice from within gave him permission to enter.

"Silence?" my mother's voice called from the kitchen.

I turned and went through the wide doorway, taking the kind of smallish steps that allowed my petticoats and skirts to sway in a ladylike way. If my mother noticed, she gave no sign.

"Have you had time to think about your rudeness?"

I nodded.

"Are you determined to behave like a proper young lady from now on?"

I nodded again.

And my heart rose a little. She didn't sound very angry now.

She waved the long-handled spoon at me. "Stir. Make yourself useful. And mind the roast chicken."

I held the copper handle tightly and stirred with intent and will, feeling my cheeks flush from the heat of the coals. I kept the chicken—which was hanging from the turning cords—at the edge of my sight. When it slowed, I used the tongs to give it another spin. The cords wound tightly, then began to unwind, turning the chicken so that it cooked without burning. When I was sure that the cords would unwind and rewind without my help for a few minutes, I concentrated on the porridge again.

Indeed. I tried to concentrate.

I kept glancing at my mother's back as she worked flour and fat into a piecrust on the baking table. She was wearing the plainest farmwife house dress imaginable. Only for balls and weddings did she wear a good wig or frizz her own hair and powder it. Her gowns were always a year or two behind. It wasn't so much her Puritan upbringing, I don't think, as her lifelong thrift that kept her from buying finery.

Anne's mother is the very vision of fashion, always, and Sarah's mother is consistently turned out very well, given her stoutness. And neither of them is as strict or as difficult as my mother. Every once in a while she turned to look at me, to see if I was idling. I was not. I would not. I knew the harder I worked at whatever tasks she set me, the sooner I would be riding Lily again.

I know it is hard for my mother to understand why Lily means so much to me. I have tried to explain and cannot. Lily's dam is one of my father's favorite mares, a sweet-natured bay. Her father is a big-boned gray stallion that belongs to Mr. Talbot. I first saw Lily the day she was born.

When I knelt beside her, she nuzzled my face, breathing into my hair. I was eight. Her color, the cream-white of spring lilies, was a surprise to everyone. She was so beautiful that I loved just looking at her. I was the first to ride Lily, Simon leading her along the barn aisle at a walk. I had spent so much time brushing her and talking to her that she didn't mind me on her back. Lily has always listened to all my secrets, all of my sorrows. I knew she would go through fire for me, and I would not hesitate to do the same for her.

CHAPTER THREE

❦ ❦ ❦

By the time I heard Father bidding his guests
good night and safe travel, I had stirred the
peas porridge into a perfect smoothness and kept
it from scorching. The chicken had browned
evenly and the whole house smelled of the drip-
pings. The mince pie was out of the bake-oven
and cooling on a sideboard.

Samuel sniffed at it as he was coming in,
and my mother made a shooing motion without
turning around. Then my father was in the wide
doorway, wearing one of his best embroidered
waistcoats, the stitches so fine that the flowers
and vines seemed nearly real. That meant the guests
had been important; he had wanted to impress them.

"There's my good girl, helping her mother," he
said. He came to kiss the top of my head, then went
to his chair. My mother brought him warmed cider

to sip while he waited for supper. I could smell the nutmeg in it, and it made my mouth water.

I watched my mother carefully from beneath my lashes, my right hand still moving the spoon. I was afraid she would suddenly clear her throat and tell my father that I had been spying on him. But she didn't. She only set about filling the bowls with soup, then lifted the chicken down and carved it on the sideboard. I carried the steaming soup bowls and set one at each place. My mother carried the broad wooden charger laden with chicken meat. I went to sit in my chair.

Samuel seemed to be looking at me whenever I glanced at him, so I stopped glancing. He can make me laugh a hundred ways, and he is just wicked enough to do it when I am intent on being serious. He can arch one brow high and swoop the other low. He can wiggle his ears. He can tighten his mouth exactly the way Mother does, except when he does it, it is funny. Funny enough that once it made me spit pudding all over the table linen. Yes, that really happened. We were at dinner, the room bright with noonday sunshine, and there were two guests at the table, merchants my father had often done business with. Imagine how my proper, serious-minded mother reacted to *that*.

And, as you may imagine, that was the last thing I wanted to do while I was trying to be perfectly good. I looked up, wishing someone would say something. Usually we talked at supper, I thought, then realized that my father and Samuel had been talking all day—and listening. I envied Samuel. I glanced up and my eyes found him.

"I missed Mr. Hampton's rebuttal," he said suddenly, and I was so grateful I smiled at him. He glanced at me, then back at Father. "Was he in accord, then? Do they all think the king has enough soldiers here to enforce the unloading of the tea?"

Father used his napkin, then laid down his knife and patted his wig, nudging it a little higher on his forehead before he answered. "They do," he said, answering Samuel, but glancing at my mother and me, too. "The colonials who have dared to engage the king's men in the past have all learned hard lessons. They would be fools to try again. Mr. Hampton, like the rest of us, thinks they will give in and pay the tea tax after a little more shouting in the taverns."

"Do you think so?" Samuel asked, and I heard an odd note in his voice. I turned to study his face as he looked at Father. It was plain as day to me. Samuel knew Father was lying.

Father took another sip of soup, then went on. "I do. I only hope this is the last of the taxation acts for a good long time." His face darkened and he glanced at Samuel for an instant, then looked away.

I stared at my porridge bowl. Why would Father fib? To ease Mother's mind? To protect me from worry over something I could not change? It had to be that. He was protecting us.

I was full of questions I didn't dare to ask for fear Mother would find my interest improper and unladylike—and I knew she would never tolerate my questioning Father's honesty about anything. I glanced at her.

She was sitting straight as a fence post, her eyes moving from my father to my brother, then back. She wasn't wearing lace anywhere this evening, and her dress was linen, not silk. Her own hair was twisted in a knot, then pinned up—no wig, no powder, nothing. The perfect country-woman. Samuel drank the last of his cider, and she stood to get more. Normally Prissy would be serving, but my mother always let her go to bed early on Mondays. Working in the washhouse is exhausting.

"There is a special spinning day coming soon. It's at the church this time," my mother said as though she felt the tension and needed to break the silence with something, anything at all. My father glanced up, nodded, then looked back at his soup.

I stared at my mother. *Spinning?* That hardly made a day special. She was always spinning. If Prissy had a single idle moment, she spun, too. So did I, sometimes. Our finished skeins of flax and woolen thread were kept in neat stacks inside old cheese hogsheads that Mother washed and scalded, the heavy wood keeping the mice out. The only thing I liked about being dragged along on spinning days was that sometimes Sarah came with her mother. Anne and her mother never came. The servants in their household did all the thread making.

Samuel finally made some polite sound about the spinning day, but he was the only one. Mother smiled at him like he had handed her roses. He told Father about the gelding's stone bruise. Then the quiet thickened, and we all ate without speaking.

When supper was finally over and my father and Samuel had gone, I immediately began my chores—and Prissy's—without my mother having to say even one word. I sand-scrubbed the baking table, banked the fire, and set the peas porridge on the edge of the hearth where it would cool, not simmer itself into an inedible lump. We would eat it at noon on the morrow I was sure, and finish it for supper tomorrow night.

"Thank you for your willing help," my mother said as we finished.

"I am sorry for—" I began, but she stopped me with one hand.

"You need not apologize. Just never do it again."

I nodded. Then I took a deep breath. "I will just run out to the barn for a moment so that I can see to Lily." I tried not to make it sound like a question, but my voice rose at the end anyway.

"No," my mother said, and her voice was hard again. "If you cared as much for your real responsibilities as you do that mare, you would be better off." She lifted her chin. "Sometimes I think that it would be best if your father just sold Lily."

My whole body went cold. I took a breath to plead with her never even to think such a thing, but she was already back about her work. I couldn't see her face to tell if she had meant it.

Shaking, I went down the hall. In my room, I took off my shoes and set them by the wall, switching them left for right so I would put them on the opposite feet on the morrow. My mother said it made them last longer. I winced as my thoughts circled back. My mother could not have meant that. Sell Lily? The idea made me ill. I got into bed without lighting my candle and pulled the covers up to my chin. I lay quietly with my eyes shut until I heard my mother open my door, lean in with her candle to make sure I was asleep, and leave. Then I lay there with my eyes open for a long time, staring at the darkened ceiling, trying not to think.

I got up and opened the shutters. The wind had dropped. I slipped on my shoes and shawl, then climbed over the sill and ran down the path. I heard Prissy cough, and the sound of her turning on her cot, as I passed the servants' quarters.

I love the barn at night. The horses are sleepy, and they sigh when they hear me pass. Lily is used to my coming and going, and she doesn't startle, even if I wake her by whispering her name. I have been slipping out of the house and coming to the barn since she was born. This night, I knew it was truly foolish, as upset as my mother seemed. I just needed to see Lily.

Old Simon sleeps like a rock. He snores, too, and the sound hides the small, soft pat of my feet on the dust. Elijah might half waken sometimes, but he never stirs on his cot, and if he knows that I come, he keeps it secret.

Lily's stall is the fourth one on the left-hand side, walking in from the wide carriage doors that face the back of the house. I breathed her name and heard her stir. A few seconds after that, I felt her sweet hay breath in my hair, then her whiskers tickled my cheek. I ran my hand over her neck. Her winter coat was thick, but soft-brushed, thanks to Elijah's good care.

I felt tears rise in my eyes, and I trembled in the dark. Not just because I was in trouble with Mother, or because I feared she might try to get Father to sell my Lily. It was because of the shouts in the parlor, too, and my father fibbing to ease my mother's mind. What would happen to all of us if there was a war?

My father's hunter whickered in the next stall, and I held very still for a moment. But old Simon's snoring went right on, and there was no sound from Elijah.

I pressed my forehead against the curved hollow between Lily's jaw and her neck until I began to shiver from the cold air. Then I leaned back. "I promise," I told her in a bare whisper. "I'll be so good that Mother never punishes us like this again."

Lily rubbed her muzzle on my shoulder and blew out a long soft breath, as though she understood and forgave me. I tiptoed out and started back toward the house. Once I was over the windowsill and inside, I undressed quickly and got into bed. I would rise early and work hard. I would keep my word.

CHAPTER FOUR

❧ ❧ ❧

I got up early the next morning, and all that followed. Prissy and I sang our way through most days. She is ten years older than I am, and she has known me as long as I have been alive. She was the one who fetched hot water to the midwife the night I was born. My father has promised to free her when she is thirty—eight more years of being a slave. By then she will be too old to marry easily, and nearly too old to have children safely. Yet she sings as she works, smiles much of the time, and is kind-hearted to my family and to Elijah and Simon. And me. Especially me.

I will be sad as well as happy when she is freed and goes off on her own. For all that she is a slave, she is the closest to a real sister I have ever had. I have always known her, all the way back to the place where my memories begin. And she is sort of a second mother in an odd way, too. I will miss her, and I will miss her songs. Most of them are old, she says, taught to her by her mother and her aunties before she was sold north.

I asked her once if she would go back to find her mother once she was free. She nodded slowly and looked into my eyes. She didn't say a single word, but there was something in her look that kept me from ever asking her any stupid questions like that again. Of course she would. She would never have *left* her mother if she'd had the choice.

On Thursday, Mother had us pick up all the rugs and lug them to the heavy wood frame in the yard. Once we had them draped over the beam, the task was to wallop them with the long-handled wire beaters, over and over—hard enough to knock all the dust out of them.

Prissy and I took turns. One of us sang a song to keep a cadence and lighten work for the other, then we traded off. I loved listening to her strong, rich voice, and I did my best to sing lively when it was my turn.

"May I give you a bit of advice?" Prissy said as we were changing places.

I turned. "About rug beating?"

She laughed and reached out to brush my hair back out of my eyes. "No. About opening your shutters so you can go out to the barn at night."

My whole body reacted, and I jerked around to face her.

"Oh, how I wish I had a looking glass right now," Prissy said. "Your eyes are as big as egg yolks."

"How did you know?" I asked in a whisper, even though I knew my mother was at the church, not in the kitchen as usual.

"That's the reason for the advice," Prissy said. "Use a bit of candle wax on those hinges. The shutters *squeak*."

"How long have you known?" I asked, barely murmuring.

She leaned toward me. "Always. Since that white filly was born. The shutters didn't squeak then, but one night you sneezed, and after that I listened. I understand why you go out there, but your mother might not. Candle wax." She kissed me on the forehead, then pointed toward her quarters. "In the wardrobe. Top shelf." I went to look in the little wardrobe in the corner of her room and found four candle stubs. She had been saving them for me. I kissed her in thanks.

I heard Prissy coughing that afternoon, but thought it was the day's worth of dust. It wasn't. By nightfall she was pink with fever and shivering with ague. The next day she lay coughing in her bed, my mother and I carrying her soups and ginger drafts and chamomile tea.

"I thank you, Miss Silence," she said, every time. "I am so sorry that you will be the one stuck doing my work."

And every time I patted her hand and told her I just wanted her feeling better as soon as possible. It was true—for two reasons. I wanted her to feel better, of course. And I missed her. The house was strange and quiet without her singing—I never could seem to sing without her, not in the same sure way that I could sing with her. And without her working beside us, my mother and I were all too able to let a day pass without exchanging more than a dozen words. Usually, Prissy was the one to care for me when I was sick. This time, it was the reverse. I tried to repay all her kindnesses, doting on her and making sure she drank broth and took her chamomile tea.

The next day was Mother's spinning day, so we were alone in the house much of the afternoon. She left me with enough work for three girls as usual, but I had somehow finished a little early. So I waxed my shutter hinges, then I went out to sit with Prissy.

"Your mother said something about the horse," Prissy whispered to me when I was settled beside her bed. "She's forbidden you the barn?"

I glanced back out the door out of habit, even though I knew my mother was gone. Then I nodded. "It started when I forgot I was to help her and left early for Mrs. Chester's lessons. Then she saw me trying to listen at the parlor door when father and his friends were talking."

Prissy frowned.

"I just want to know more about the trouble," I said.

She tipped her head to one side. "Whatever for, Miss Silence? What in the world can you do about any of it? Kings and generals and the prominent men like your father—it is their business, not ours."

I exhaled. She was saying almost exactly what my mother had said many times. And I knew it was true. What could I do about any of it?

"The tavern louts and the Sons of Liberty are always upset about something the king has done," Prissy said softly, looking at the wall past my left shoulder. "They have come to blows before;

there have been shots fired, then they stopped. It will stop this time, too." She reached out and squeezed my hand. "And your mother knows how you love that mare. She won't keep you from her for too long."

I nodded, then felt a wash of remorse. Prissy was sick, and we were talking about my troubles? I straightened her bedding and wiped her face with the damp cloth I had brought. "Mother says you are feeling better?"

She nodded and patted my hand. "I am. The cough has abated. I slept through most of last night."

"Daughter?" my mother called from the back door as she came in.

I stood straight and smoothed my apron. "I will come back when I can," I told Prissy.

She smiled again and closed her eyes. "I will try to be better by morning."

But she wasn't.

It took three long days of scrubbing my hands raw keeping up with Prissy's work and my own to convince my mother that I was taking her words about helping more to heart. I didn't even try to look cheerful. Prissy was still sick, which worried me, and I was afraid to go out to the barn to see Lily, even after I had waxed the hinges. If my mother ever saw me sneaking around after dark, she would be furious and that would be that. I was afraid that she *would* speak to Father about selling Lily.

Finally one afternoon, as we finished washing the walls in the hallway, my mother began chatting with me. She asked about Mrs. Chester's instruction and if Anne was still learning both harpsichord and flute. Then she said, "Prissy is much improved. I think we are safe in leaving the day's extra work here." She gestured at the clean walls and the bucket of hot water. "She should be back at her chores on the morrow."

I nodded, keeping my somber expression.

"I have to take thread to the weaver and one of your father's perukes to be cleaned," she said. "Do you wish to come with me?"

"Yes," I said, straightening up, hoping I was making the right choice. She might assume that a ride in the carriage was important to me, that it would make me happier. I wanted her to realize that I was never happy unless I could ride Lily. It was true. Galloping Lily made me feel like I could fly, and it eased my heart in a way that nothing else did.

"Silence?"

I came out of my thoughts to find Mother looking at me.

"Go change your dress, Silence," she said. "You are spotted with soot and soap. You will want heavier stockings and your brown shawl, too. It's cold."

I ran to my room and washed and changed, then hurried back down the hall, shivering, the edges of my hair still damp from the icy water in my washbasin. My mother was nowhere to be seen, which meant she was still in her chambers. I stood close by the hearth for a moment to warm myself, then ran to the barn, pulling my shawl tight around my shoulders. Simon had the carriage ready. He waited while I ran in to talk to Lily—she was very happy to see me, nickering and tossing her head. I scratched her ears and let her nibble at my hair for a moment, then I ran out.

"How is Samuel's gelding?" I asked Simon as we both got up on the driver's bench. He shrugged. "It always takes longer than I like. But each day it's a little better."

"Will he be all right?"

Simon nodded and smiled at me. "Should be." Then he reined in at the front door and I leaped down and ran inside, calling my mother.

She appeared in the hallway, with my father's peruke box dangling from its heavy cord around her right wrist and a coach blanket beneath her left arm. Simon nodded his graying head when we came out, and my mother bade him load the hogshead barrels that held the spun thread. She waited patiently—Simon's step had slowed with age.

He arranged the containers, then closed the lid on the carriage trunk. My mother smiled at him, and I could see the affection between them. My mother had inherited Simon from her mother, and I knew she cared very much for him for that reason and because he was so honest and so loyal to her. Simon had been part of her girlhood the way Elijah and Prissy were part of mine and Samuel's.

Simon helped Mother up, then turned to me, smiling. He made a show of offering his arm. I rested my hand upon his sleeve, then jumped onto the little iron step and settled onto the bench across from my mother.

She had washed her face, too, and had put on a simple wig and changed to an elegant skirt of deep green. Her hands were red from all our washing, and she kept them in her lap, folded and resting on the heavy woolen cloth of her skirt.

She looked young for her thirty-nine years. Her mother had lived to almost fifty-seven. I hope to have as long a life.

When my mother noticed my looking at her, she smiled. "Is something troubling you, daughter?"

I shook my head.

"Pull your cap closer."

I made sure my hair was tucked beneath the thick woolen cap and worked it down over my ears. She arranged the blanket to cover both our laps.

"We are ready, Simon," she called.

Sitting back on the driver's bench, he half turned and ducked his head to show he had heard her. Then he flicked the carriage whip lightly across the horses' backs, letting the long, knotted strings slide across their slick coats without any force at all. The team of chestnut mares started off smartly, their hooves clopping on the ground as the wheels lurched into motion. I grabbed the rail with one hand.

At the bottom of Frog Lane, the cross street was full of carriages and wagons. I wished I could tell Simon to slow a little as we passed the ordinaries where men were talking. As it was, I could gather only a word here and there, but the voices almost all sounded angry. And I noticed that the red-coated British soldiers were standing apart, in groups. It scared me and chilled me. I followed close on my mother's heels as we went around the hitching rail and stepped up onto the boardwalk.

The peruke maker's shop was quiet, warm, and smelled of the pomades and oils he used in his trade. Mr. Williams winked at me as he always did and gestured to a bowl of comfits on the shelf beside his cash box. I sidled closer and took two of the sugared walnuts, watching my mother and hoping she wouldn't notice. No one knew how old Mr. Williams was, but my own parents had known him when they were children.

I loved the comfits, but what I loved best was Mr. Williams. He always wore velvet breeches and had lace hanging from his jacket sleeves, and his shoes were bootblacked and shined. And he always had on an elaborate wig. It was his trademark; he was always dressed for a ball.

Most of the wigs he made *were* elaborate, and expensive, made especially for whoever ordered them. He made wigs for most of the merchants in town—including my own father. Sarah's and Anne's fathers both bought their wigs here, and Anne's mother had Mr. Williams make truly extravagant ones.

I walked to the far wall and looked at the wooden dolls lined up on the shelf. They came from Paris every year, shipped in special boxes, each one dressed in the newest fashions, stockings to wigs. My mother's dressmaker always had them on display, too, so people could see the new fashions and make their choices. This year's female dolls wore wigs that had tall, arching pillows of hair that swooped upward from the brow to an unnatural height, then fell, just as abruptly, into stiff curls that flattened themselves against the back of the head and ended in a straight fall that covered the back of the neck.

The male dolls wore simpler wigs, but the high crowns were there, too. I knew my father would buy a new one, high and fluffy like these. I knew my mother would, too, even though she thought it was silly. My father let her save money on gowns—the styles changed more slowly anyway. Out-of-style wigs were another matter. It would be noticed and gossiped about on any woman, especially the wife of a wealthy man.

"When will he need the wig back?" Mr. Williams asked my mother.

"No hurry," my mother said politely. "This week or next, no matter. He is wearing the major bob more often now, anyway."

Mr. Williams nodded and made a note in his ledger, then he looked up. "Will the young master Samuel be needing a larger minor bob soon?"

My mother sighed. "It is likely. And perhaps something more formal—he is rising sixteen this year. I will let you know."

Mr. Williams laid down his quill and carried the wig box into the back room. He came back out with a farewell sweetmeat for me. "In two or three years, you will be the one needing ballroom wigs," he whispered as he handed it to me. My mother frowned, but I took it from him. I thanked him politely before I followed her out the door.

"Pass along the waterfront," my mother told Simon. "We will take some air before we go to the weaver's."

Simon pulled the team to the right, following Summer Street down to Belcher's Lane. I held my breath. There was nothing unusual about my mother wanting to go this way. She always liked to see if any of Father's ships were in port, their holds full of cloth, tools, glassware, and all else from England—or whale oil and molasses from the southern islands. He had started with one ship and had made enough money within a few years to buy several more. He had once imported tea, too, before the king had made it illegal for any company besides the East India Company to do so.

It was a little cold for my mother's usual carriage ride to spot my father's ships, though. Was she curious about the East India Company ships, too? As we got closer and the road curved with the shoreline, I looked for any of Father's four ships, even though they usually came in farther down, past the old wharf. When I didn't see them, I looked out over the water toward the shipping lane between Noddles Island and the swampy end of Dorchester Flats. There were two ships headed in, and one going out.

I had never been on a ship coming into or going out of Boston. Samuel had, of course, with Father. And when Father had asked him to learn the depths and the course of the shipping lanes, I had helped him study the maps.

There were two main lanes, both dotted with islands and shallow places. There are more islands than you'd think just looking offshore. Samuel had had to memorize the list. Thompson's, Spectacle, Castle, Moon's, Hangman, Long, Rainsforth . . . and so on. But then, Boston was on a spit of land that was almost an island itself.

I took a long breath and scanned the harbor again—and I saw them. There. Off Griffin's Wharf—three ships with the East India flag. It was the easiest banner to spot in the harbor with its British Union canton in the upper corner and the blazing, slanted, red and white stripes.

As we got closer, I could see the sailors in their wide-legged pants climbing the rigging—the captain probably had them scrubbing wood and repairing rope while they waited to unload the cargo. My father's captains rarely allowed an idle moment for the men on his ships, I knew.

"There they are," my mother said quietly.

It startled me, and I turned to look at her. "What?"

"You know very well what I mean," she said.

I nodded and looked back at the harbor. One of the ships was angled away from us. I could see the name on the stern: *Dartmouth.* Mother and I said nothing more as the carriage rolled past Griffin's Wharf and went on. It was then that I heard the shouting. My mother turned the instant I did. There was a crowd of men coming down a side street toward the wharves. They were talking in loud, angry voices, which were tangled into a knot that I could not unravel into anything meaningful. More men joined them as they came, falling into step. I was astounded. There were *dozens* of men, perhaps a hundred. Simon touched the whip to the horses' backs, and they broke into a trot. I stared as the angry-faced men came toward us.

My mother pinched my arm. "Mind your own affairs, Silence." I lowered my head, but I could hear the men yelling as we passed Anthorpe's and Rowe's wharves. Simon urged the mares faster. I could hear Mother humming one of Prissy's tunes. Was she scared? I was. Some of the men were carrying muskets. My mother suddenly leaned forward. "Simon?"

He half turned, his chin tucked and his right ear toward her.

"Take us straight to the weaver now. And avoid the crowd if you can."

"Yes, ma'am," he said politely. He pulled the team to the left and rounded a corner, taking us into the maze of narrow streets above the wharves. I knew he had meant to leave the shouting crowds behind, but there were men walking here, too, their faces grim and strained, their voices raised, all of them heading toward Griffin's Wharf. Because the crowds were thinner here, I could understand some of what they were saying. It was the tea tax—and King George—they were angry at.

"King Georgie thinks he rules the world, Boston Harbor, and all the heavens, too!" a man near us shouted across the street to friends. They laughed. It was a sharp sound, not a merry one.

Simon turned the carriage down a lane with merchant shops and bakeries. I could smell the day's bread even as the shouts faded behind us. Then a ragged pack of younger boys bolted across the street, startling the horses. Simon shouted at them. They just laughed and gathered into a loose circle. I heard a shout, then a shot. Or at least it sounded like a shot. The circle of boys was suddenly silent. Then the tallest one started off running in the direction from which the sound had come. The others followed.

I glanced at my mother. Her mouth was a tight line, and she looked angry now, not scared. "Ruffians," she said quietly, and there was scorn in her voice.

I glanced back and saw more young men sprinting toward the waterfront. They were all dressed in good clothes, and I saw more than one with silver buckles on his shoes. My mother was staring straight ahead when I glanced at her.

Ahead of us, a group of British soldiers was marching around the corner and onto the lane we were following. I saw a boy with silver buttons on his shirt pick up a fist-sized stone. Then Simon rounded another corner, and I could no longer see. Had the boy been foolish enough to throw a stone at the king's soldiers? What would his father do if he was caught and arrested? Disown his son? Probably. I knew my father would.

⁂ ⁂ ⁂

That night I could not sleep and lay awake wondering how many fathers and sons would come to hate one another before all the trouble was solved—if it ever was. My worries ran in circles until I gave up trying to sleep and finally slipped out to the barn. Lily whickered when she heard me. Simon's snores went on, unabated. Elijah stirred but didn't waken, as usual. I leaned against Lily's warm shoulder and tangled my hands in her mane and thought about all the angry men. And then I cried. Lily stood motionless, her muzzle fitting into the curve of my neck, her whickers tickling my skin. And as always, it comforted me simply to love her and to have her love me.

The next morning, Simon took me to Anne's house for Mrs. Chester's lessons. The best part of the morning was when Anne's older brother came

53

into the parlor with a friend, not knowing that we were there. His friend nodded politely when Mrs. Chester made us all introduce ourselves. "I've seen you riding," Alain Bonnet said to me. "You're as good as any boy ever was." He smiled and hesitated, then ducked his head. "And far prettier."

I felt my cheeks go pink, and I saw Anne's hand fly up to her mouth. Then Mrs. Chester stepped in and shooed the boys out so we could go back to learning how to fold napkins and set a beautiful table.

When it was time to go, Anne and Sarah followed me to the door. "Alain is very shy," Anne whispered. "And very nice."

I kept blushing, all the way home, every time I thought about what Alain had said. But no one noticed at all when I came in—my cheeks were rosy from the chill, too. That night I went out to the barn again. I was scared my mother would see me, and I knew I shouldn't disobey her, but it felt like everything was changing, in the colonies, in Boston, and inside me, too—and being around Lily eased my worries. "And I think there is a boy who likes me," I told her once I had finished reciting my concerns. She nudged me with her muzzle, and I smiled.

CHAPTER FIVE

🎭 🎭 🎭

*S*oon after that, my mother woke me before dawn. Prissy was in the kitchen when I got there, and it was lovely to have her company again. We used the lifting stick to move the kettle of steaming water to one side so I could build a new fire on the red coals from the night before. We both shivered as the flames flickered to life, laughing when our teeth chattered. Then my mother interrupted our foolishness.

"We are going to do a thorough cleaning," my mother told us, carrying out an armful of rags. "Get the buckets, Prissy, please." Prissy nodded and bustled off to the hall pantry. I stared at my mother. Her face was as grim as it had been the day before, watching the boys making fun of the king. She glanced at me so sharply I looked away, but I could tell that whatever was upsetting her, it was not Prissy or me.

"Start in the parlor," she said to Prissy. "Walls, floors, then oil the table and the chairs and the chair rail. Don't overdo. Sit and rest when you must."

"Begin in your own room," she said to me. "I want it spotless. Then the kitchen. Wait for the water to boil, then get started."

I nodded again. Prissy was lining up three buckets. The hot water boiled within minutes on the new, roaring fire, and I used the big ladle to fill each bucket halfway with scalding water from the deep iron pot. I heard Lily whinny from the road, and I turned to stare in that direction. Was Elijah leading her out for exercise?

"Keep your mind on your work," my mother said sternly. Then her face softened a little. "Your father is having Elijah take her along when he exercises some of the others."

I nodded, relieved and hurt, in an odd way. I was the one who should be exercising her. But I was stuck inside cleaning. Why? The house was already clean. But my mother's face was hard and stern again, and I did not say a word of what I felt. Instead, I helped Prissy grate the soap and stir the wash water until the slivers dissolved. Then

I picked up my pail. The soap smelled so sharp my eyes watered.

There is little that is glorious about cleaning a house. I swept my room thoroughly, using the coarse broom, then the fine one. I washed the floors, then rubbed beeswax into the wood with a scrub brush. This is an old family secret, or so my mother claims, handed down through the women in her family. It does make the floor shine and it does preserve the wood, but it breaks the back of the woman—or the girl—doing it.

I could hear Prissy singing down the hall, and for that I was grateful. I had missed it dearly in the days she had been sick. Her voice rose and fell as prettily as a bird flies. I knew all her songs, and, as usual, I sang with her as I worked.

By the time I was finished in my room, Samuel and Father were up and about. Prissy made them breakfast while I cleaned out the ash bin. When I took the bucket outside to scatter the sooty grit over my mother's frozen garden plot, I heard Lily whinny from the barn. So Elijah had her back, safe and sound.

I hoped Samuel's gelding would heal fast. A year before, that would have been my brother's biggest worry. But now, I barely saw him except at mealtimes—and then he and Father were either debating about what the king might do if the tea wasn't unloaded, or they were tense and silent, both lost in thought.

I went back into the house and helped Prissy cook. I told her about Alain and what he had said. She waggled a finger at me. "Don't be in a hurry for young men's attention," she said, smiling.

"I'm not," I promised. "It just . . . surprised me."

Prissy put her arms around me. "Plenty of boys are going to notice how pretty you are," she said. "Wait for the one who notices something else."

I nodded, and she stepped back, smiling. "He said I rode well," I told her.

We both laughed, and then we went back to work before my mother had time to notice that we were idling.

"I have business with the financiers," my father told my mother as he finished eating. He pushed his charger back and wiped his sticky hands on the damp napkin she brought him. I saw Samuel looking at me, and so I met his stare, but with my eyes crossed. He laughed. Father shot him a look, and Samuel pointed at me. "Her fault. Making faces. Again."

My mother caught my father's eye. He rose, and they went into the hallway to talk. I could only hope it wasn't about me, but perhaps it was. A little knot formed in my stomach. Had she heard me going out to the barn at night? There had been no anger in Mother's voice when she chided Samuel. She adores him. I know she loves me, too, but sometimes she forgets to be kind to me. She never forgets with him. I know why.

Samuel is her first child, in a way, but there is far more to it than that. There were two before him who did not pass their first year. And Samuel was sickly, too. My mother has never said much about caring for him except that she rarely slept. I can imagine her, taking care of a small, weak baby the way she does all things. With a fury. I am sure she did it better than anyone ever had—than anyone ever could.

And she saved him. At about five months old, Samuel just stopped crying and began to grow. I have heard that part of the story a hundred times. My parents had meant to have a bigger family than the two of us. There are four empty bedchambers upstairs to prove it. When I was born, my mother was ready to save me, too, but I nursed like a piglet and never cried and grew like a weed in the sun. So she says, anyway. And after me, there were no more babies, frail or strong. My mother accepted her small family as God's will—what else could she do?

I glanced out the door. Mother was talking in a very low voice, a serious look on her face. Samuel was not looking at them. He was reaching to ladle more samp onto his charger. Staring at the steaming corn pudding made my mouth water. I knew that Sam was so used to Mother doting on him that he didn't even notice it. I admit I was jealous, sometimes.

"Are you finished, Sam?" my father asked, coming back to the doorway.

Samuel laid down the ladle and stood up. "I am."

"Tell Simon to bring the carriage around, then."

My brother nodded and paced out of the kitchen in long strides. We all watched him go, and I wondered if we were thinking the same thing. He was so *big* all of a sudden. He was taller than Father.

We all three went back to work. It was late afternoon when we finished, and my back ached. My mother and Prissy fell into their usual conversation about household matters as we sipped mint tea in the kitchen. And then the surprise came.

My mother looked at me and said, "You have done good work this day, Silence. Run out to the barn, will you, and tell Elijah that his mistress wants to be sure he polishes the harness well when the carriage returns."

"Yes, ma'am," I managed. And I had my dirty apron off in an eyeblink and was on my way.

Lily was so glad to see me with the sun still up! She whickered and put her head over the rail so that I could scratch her ears. She blew out a breath that tickled my neck and lifted my hair. I laughed. I rubbed her ears—which she loves—and I was lost in a daydream about our next gallop across the Common when I remembered my errand. I was pretty sure that Elijah already knew to polish the harness—that my mother had just done me a kindness in sending me out—but I wasn't positive.

"Elijah?" I called, expecting an answer. There was none. I pitched my voice higher and louder. "Elijah?" I waited, then walked out the side doors to look in the paddocks. He wasn't there, either. I tried to remember another time in my life when Elijah had been neither in the barn nor the paddock if he was not off helping my father load bags of corn or something else into the hard-wheeled freight wagon. I could not. He was probably in the privy behind the hedgerow. I went back to rubbing Lily's ears.

Then, after a long moment, I went into her stall and leaned against her shoulder. I was cold, and I had not brought my shawl, thinking I would be in the barn only a few minutes. I was not fool enough to think that my mother was giving me the rest of the day to linger. I called Elijah, twice more, then looked in the tack room to be sure he had not fallen asleep there—or in the haystack. Then I walked the path toward the privy, meaning simply to call out my mother's message, then leave. But the privy door was standing open. He was not there, either.

Confounded, I stopped and tried to think. I used to find him napping now and then in the grain bins when we were both small. So I went to look, even though I knew he was far too big to fit in the tin boxes now.

What I found confounded me further. Neatly folded and laid on top of the oats and cracked corn there were roughly made trousers and a shirt from brown cloth, cut like the buckskin clothing the Indian men wore. There was a little cloth sack lying beside them. I pulled the drawstring open far enough to see a headband, with turkey feathers sewn into it.

I heard voices, and, without thinking, I folded the strange costume and put it back into the grain bin, then ran to Lily's stall. Seconds later, the clopping of hooves got louder, and I heard my father's voice as the carriage stopped in the dusty alley that runs along the far side of the barn beneath a row of oak trees. "Thank you for your help, Elijah," I heard him say.

Elijah made some answer, then I heard the team start forward; a moment later, he came through the wide barn doors on the far end of the barn. He was whistling, but he stopped when he saw me.

"My mother asked me to tell you to polish the harness," I said, trying to imagine what in the world he was doing with an Indian costume. It most certainly didn't belong to gray-haired Simon. Was he going to be in a play of some kind? He nodded to show he had heard me. "Tell her I will," he said. Then he smiled. "Just as I always do." I smiled back at him. I had been right. My mother had been kind.

The next day, once work was finished, Mother and Prissy were shelling walnuts, an easy task. My mother looked at me. "Why don't you take Lily out onto the lane for a quick gallop." My heart stopped, then started again. I blinked. My mother smiled. "Go. There is little light left."

I could not stand still while Simon got the sidesaddle on Lily. He lifted me up, then stood back, arching his brows, pretending to be afraid that we would gallop right over him. I laughed and pivoted Lily in a close circle, then guided her toward the big double doors that faced the lane.

My spirits soaring, excited to gallop, I spent the first few moments doing what my father had taught me. I arranged my skirt so that there was only one layer of cloth between my right leg and the curved saddle tree and none at all bunched around my right foot where I tucked it beneath my left leg. I made sure the single stirrup was squared and that my riding boot was centered in it. Then, ready to pull my foot free of the stirrup if I had to, I rocked lightly in the saddle to make sure Lily hadn't held her breath while Simon tightened the cinch. If the saddle had loosened and I didn't notice until we were galloping, my weight could make it slide, carrying me beneath Lily's belly—and my crossed legs would make it almost impossible to free myself from the saddle.

Once I was settled, I leaned forward a bit and took a deep breath of pure joy. Then I gave Lily her head. She leaped into a canter, tossing her mane. I held her in until she settled into her stride, then let her out just enough to gallop down the lane, her tail and my hair like flags in the wind. I had a hard time reining her in at the bottom of the hill, but I managed a wide, sweeping turn, then crossed the road again, passing in front of a dray wagon. The wagoneer gave me a friendly shout, and I lifted a hand in thanks as he reined in a little to let us fly past.

I let Lily gallop flat out on the way back up the lane, past our barn doors, and down to the edge of the Common. I had to haul back on the reins to slow her enough to make the turn, and then we pounded back up the slope. I threw back my head and laughed, tears on my cheeks, then leaned forward to hug Lily's neck for a stride or two before I sat upright again. Happy for the first time in what felt like an eternity, I galloped Lily up and down the lane twelve times, until she slowed to a collected canter on her own. Then we went the same route twice more, rocking along, like one being, in perfect rhythm.

By the time I took her back to the barn, she was winded and calm—and so was I. Elijah lifted me down and took the reins. "I'll walk her cool," he said, and for the first time, I noticed his voice was getting squeaky-deeper just as Sam's had last year. He smiled at me. I wanted to ask him about the costume, but before I could say anything, he shook his head. "Hurry. If you get back in before it's dark, maybe your mother will let you do this again tomorrow evening." I thanked him, and my heart was dancing all the way up the path to the house.

As I went in, I heard Father and Samuel talking in the kitchen. Mother was stirring the peas porridge, looking upset. Father's face was strained, his voice tight as he bade me good evening. I looked from him to Samuel, then back. "What happened?"

Samuel swallowed and looked at me, holding my eyes and making sure he didn't glance at either of our parents. I knew why a moment later. He wanted to tell me, and they would have stopped him.

"There was a meeting today, men from all over Suffolk County. They tried to talk to Governor Hutchinson, to ask him to consider their concerns about the tax on the tea. He said he'd talk later, but then he went out to Milton, without speaking to anyone." Sam paused and swallowed, and my father lifted one hand to keep him from going on.

"No," my mother said, and I turned to stare at her. "Please let him tell us."

My father hesitated, then he spoke. "The king has promised the East India Company his protection," he said. "If the rebels don't willingly let the ships unload the tea, His Majesty's warships will open their cannons upon Boston."

"War?" I whispered, looking at Samuel. I was afraid to ask my father.

Samuel didn't answer.

It was my father who filled the silence again. "If this goes much further, I cannot think what else to call it. These so-called Sons of Liberty are fools. They think they want *liberty*? Without the protection of the English crown, we'll have invaders from every corner of the earth coming ashore. We cannot protect ourselves."

He fell silent, and I heard my mother take in a breath, then sigh it out. After a long moment, Father pushed his wig higher on his forehead and seemed to gather himself. "No men of sound mind are going to push the king into war. It would be madness." Then my parents stood up and went into the hall to talk.

CHAPTER SIX

✵ ✵ ✵

*S*amuel and I sat at the table and stared into the orange-red coals of the unbanked hearth fire. King George was a months-long sea voyage away. How long would it take before more of his soldiers arrived? Three months? Five? It would depend on the weather and the Parliament and whatever else was worrying the King of England.

England.

My parents had both grown up there. My mother's stories of royals in bright silk and tatted lace riding in carriages with silver fittings had always seemed impossible, like a fairy's tale to make children's eyes go wide. She had actually seen King George twice when she was a girl.

If it was going to be dangerous here, would we leave Boston? Would Father want to take us back to London? He had two brothers and a dozen cousins there. One had visited when I was four or five. Mother's whole family would be delighted to have her back. I had never met any of them, but they wrote once a year. Would Father sell the horses rather than subject them to the long sea voyage? I felt my whole body stiffen. He might.

"Silence?" Samuel whispered.

I looked at him. "What?"

"You have to promise me you will be careful."

I nodded, then shook my head. "What does that mean, Sam? Stay in the house? We are not so far from the harbor that a cannonball might not—"

"Don't scare yourself." he interrupted me. "I don't think it will come to that."

I stared at him. "How can you say that? Is that what Father thinks?"

He nodded. "It is. He said so. He doesn't think that Hutchinson is foolish enough to provoke a fight, no matter what King George has said about using cannons."

I shook my head. "Mother and I saw men in the streets, Samuel. They were so angry." Samuel turned his head and was quiet for so long that I stood up and washed the cups in the basin. When I turned around, he was staring at me.

"You have always been a good sister to me," he said slowly.

"And you are the best brother anyone could ask for," I told him, wondering why he would choose this evening, this moment, to say such a thing. And then I realized that he must be scared, too, scared that we might die in the night and he didn't want his life to end without having—

"Silence," he said suddenly, leaning close, "Father and I heard the arguments at the meeting in the church for hours before we went on with his errands."

I stared at him. "What did they say?"

He shrugged. "They make a very good case that the tea tax is unfair, even illegal. Father's financial partners agree, but then, some of them have a stake in the tea imports."

I waited, expecting him to explain that loyalty to the king was more important than a few pennies paid in taxes. But he only stood up and paced to the hearth, then back.

"Samuel?"

My father's voice startled us both. Sam stopped midstep. "Yes, Father?"

"Your mother is worried. Will you run out and wake Elijah and ask him to harness the sorrel carriage team? Tell him to knot the reins up out of the way, then just turn the mares into their stalls. Then go to bed yourself. Nothing is going to happen until Hutchinson comes back and answers the demands of the meeting."

Samuel nodded. I knew my father was trying to assure my mother that we could flee at a moment's notice if we had to. Samuel stood up and went past our father, out the door. I could hear his boots on the wooden floor as he walked down the hall.

"Silence," my father said, "get to your bed."

I shook my head. "I don't think I am going to be able to sleep."

He nodded, a big, exaggerated gesture, like an adult would give an argumentative three-year-old. "Yes, you will, dear. Just close your eyes, and before you know it tomorrow will have come."

I blinked, realizing something. I did the work of a grown woman beside Mother and Prissy all day every day, but he still thought of me as a little girl. As if to confirm my thoughts, he reached out and patted the top of my head as he turned to leave. Then he hesitated and turned back. "If there is anything to frighten you in the night," he said, "come into our chamber. I cannot imagine your mother sleeping tonight either, though you both should try."

I nodded and watched him walk away. Then I just stood still for a long time, staring into the fire. I heard the door open and close and knew that Samuel was back inside. He didn't come talk—he went straight to his bedchamber. After another long moment, I lit a candle and carried it to my room. I set it on my washstand and sat on the edge of my bed, trying to still my fear—but I could not. I got up and paced to the window and back. I wanted, more than anything, to run out to the barn and spend a few more moments with Lily before I tried to sleep. I waited until there was no other sound in the house, until I was sure Elijah had had time to harness two horses, then go back to bed. Then I got up and ran to the window.

Going into the barn, I heard Simon's familiar snoring. He, at least, would get some rest this night. I stood just inside the doors, waiting for my eyes to adjust to the darkness. Once I could see that Elijah was on his cot, I tiptoed past the harnessed carriage mares, standing quietly in their stalls, and then stopped in front of Lily's. She shook her mane and stamped her foreleg, then paced another circle.

"I didn't mean to startle you," I whispered, knowing the late night commotion had made her uneasy.

She lowered her head and blew out a breath against my cheek. For a long moment we stood perfectly still like that, with her breath tickling my ear, her warm muzzle resting on my shoulder. I reached up and made sure she had a halter on. I wanted to put her saddle and bridle over the stall gate—for the same reason my mother had wanted the carriage team harnessed—to save time if we all woke up to the sound of cannon this night. But if I tried to make my way to the tack room and back in the dark, I would almost certainly wake Simon. Elijah might be willing to keep my secret, but Simon would not. His loyalty was to my mother.

Lily suddenly raised her head and whickered, low. I held my breath. Simon's snoring went on, like a clock ticking. Elijah did not stir. "I have to go," I whispered to Lily. She rubbed her forehead against my shoulder, and I braced myself against the shoving. I kissed her muzzle when she lifted her head again.

"I won't let anything hurt you," I murmured, even though I knew it was a promise I couldn't keep. I *wanted* to. "Father will make sure we are all safe," I added, and I had at least some small faith in that. I knew he would try.

Heading back to the house, I decided to leave on all but my dress and petticoats, to be ready to run if it came to that. I draped them over my chair back, and set my shoes nearby, where I could find them in the dark if I had to. I had no striker and no hearth with coals to relight the candle, so I let it burn a long time before I finally blew it out.

Then I lay awake listening to the sound of my own heart. I imagined the booming of cannons every time the wind rose enough to rattle the shutters. I thought I heard shouts in the distance, then realized that it was the sound of the shutter latch creaking a little when the wind pushed hard against it. Were Anne and Sarah both lying awake? Had their fathers and brothers told them about what had happened?

I dozed off. I am not sure how long I slept. It was still dark when something woke me. I opened my shutters and stood before my window. I heard an uneasy whinny from the barn; it was Lily. I ran to put my stockings on—the floor was like ice. Then I shrugged on my dress—not bothering with my petticoats—buttoned my shoes, and eased open my bedroom door. The house was silent. There were no voices, not a whisper of movement. No one else was up. I closed the door and turned toward my window. I would just make sure that Lily was all right, then come back. I had no intention of adding to my mother's worries, only to ease my own.

The shutters opened silently. Once I was outside, I began to shiver and wished I had gotten my shawl. When I opened the barn door—slowly, as always, to keep it from banging—I saw Lily lift her head. I waited, listening, as usual. Simon's snoring was loud and even. I ran, light-footed, past the harnessed mares to Lily's stall gate. Then I stopped, startled.

Elijah lowered the curry comb and stared at me. He had a lantern sitting low on the stall floor, the flame turned down so there was just enough light to see that Lily's coat was matted with sweat. There was a groom's rag draped over the gate. He had dried her as much as he could before he'd started brushing. Steam was rising from her coat in the cold air.

"What are you doing?" I demanded.

Elijah started to speak, then closed his mouth. His right hand came up in a gesture that meant nothing, then he lowered it and looked away. Simon's snores got louder, then quieted again.

"Answer me!" I said, keeping my voice to a hissing whisper.

"I woke up early, so I thought I would just—"

"Have you been riding her?" I interrupted.

He lowered his head and then looked up at me again.

I clenched my teeth. "*Have* you?"

I think he was about to answer when Lily tossed her head and nickered. The rhythm of Simon's snores faltered again, and then resumed as Elijah and I stared at each other in the dim light of the lantern.

"Get that lantern up on the hook," I said between my teeth. "If you bump it you could burn down the barn."

Elijah obeyed me, glancing toward the little alcove where Simon slept. Then he went back to brushing out Lily's damp coat.

"I will tell my father," I said.

Elijah nodded without turning.

"You will be punished."

He nodded again.

"Where did you go? And why?"

He didn't answer me, but Simon's snoring hesitated again, and I heard him turn over on his cot.

"Tell me!" I whispered.

Elijah was working his way from Lily's near-side shoulder to her flank. He made long, practiced sweeps with the brush. He didn't speak, and he didn't look at me. His shoulders were squared, high, like someone expecting a blow.

I dug my fingernails into the wooden gate. "Elijah? Answer me!" Then I realized that maybe my father had asked him to ride to the harbor. "Did my father tell you to go somewhere?"

He was silent, brushing the sweat-damp winter coat on Lily's shoulders and back.

"Elijah, please. If you don't give me an answer, I will have to tell him."

He glanced up at me and nodded, and didn't say a word.

I whirled and ran back to the house, so angry that I was shaking. Galloping my Lily in the dark? What if she had broken a leg? Horses do not survive that, ever. My father once had his favorite hunter stumble and go down hard enough to break a foreleg just above the pastern. Father had no choice. He shot the horse to spare it the misery of dying slowly. I imagined Lily's trusting eyes full of pain, and the image was so terrible that it shoved aside all my worries about the king's orders and cannons and tea. Jaw clenched and stiff with anger, I slid over my windowsill and slipped into my petticoats and an apron. Still furious, I opened the door to the hall. But then I hesitated.

No matter what my father had said, they would not be expecting me to knock on their chamber door this night. I could not think of a single time in my life when I had awakened my parents. If I woke them now, they would assume I had actually *heard* cannons, or that something else was terribly wrong. My mother's heart would fly into her throat, and it would be a long time before I could even explain to them what was wrong—first I would have to explain that I had been out in the barn.

I shook my head. Elijah had never done anything wicked enough to merit punishment worse than a mild scolding. Why was I assuming he would simply take one of our horses and gallop off in the night for no reason? And if I ran into my parent's room, startling them awake, admitting that I had slipped out of the house without permission and he had only been obeying my father's instructions . . . ? Stewing in the bitter juice of my impossible situation, I sat on the edge of my bed until I was so cold that I had to get under the covers. Then I slept fitfully until my mother knocked on my door.

I opened my eyes to see her face lit by the candle, the rest of her invisible in the near dark. "Get dressed and come to the kitchen. Samuel and your father have been down to the harbor. He says there is terrible news."

CHAPTER SEVEN

✹ ✹ ✹

*M*y mother herded me along like a farmwife driving geese. If she had noticed
that I was already dressed, she said nothing. My
father's face was tight and angry. When he saw me,
he gestured impatiently for me to sit down. I joined my mother at the table. Samuel was standing
by the sunny window, looking upward at the ceiling as my father began to speak. It was well past
dawn. I had slept late.

"I can't know yet how serious this will become,
but I want you both to know that I will do whatever
I can to protect you, whatever comes."

"What happened last night?" my mother
asked.

He exhaled. "A band of hotheads did something ridiculous."

I glanced at my mother. Her eyes were fastened on my father's face. She nodded curtly. "What? What have they done?"

My father shook his head. "They destroyed the tea."

My mother leaned forward, incredulous, her brow wrinkled. "How?"

My father waved one hand, like someone shooing flies. His face was tense, and he kept glancing at the ceiling, then back at us.

"How?" my mother repeated.

"They were well ordered about it," my father said. "They rowed into the harbor, three companies of men in three boats, one for each ship. They came close silently, then climbed aboard. They broke up the packing chests and threw them into the water. The captains are merchants, not soldiers, and had no wish to fight. I suspect that fool Samuel Adams was involved, but no one can prove it."

My mother glanced at me. I knew what she was thinking. Father had brought tea from India back when the king allowed anyone to import it. Tea was expensive. Shipping it across the sea cost a great deal. "*All* of it was ruined?" my mother asked, but Father was thinking his own thoughts.

"How will King George react?" my father finally whispered. Then his voice rose. "These fools court war and disaster, all to save a few shillings on a box of tea."

"Why was this allowed?" my mother asked. "We saw ruffians, Silence and I, when we were about our errands. But we saw king's men, and they wouldn't allow—"

"It isn't so much that anyone *allowed* it, Mother," Samuel said from the doorway. "No one could stop it. Eight or nine thousand men gathered to hear Sam Adams explain that the king's governor wouldn't let them send the ships back to England, that the tea taxes had to be paid. Some of them came back in the night to watch the tea thrown into the water. It took hours. There were three hundred odd tea chests and—"

"Some of that is probably an exaggeration, Samuel," Father said tightly. "But there were men on the bay this morning, thirty or more boats." He looked at my mother. "We saw that ourselves." My mother closed her eyes and opened them again as though she wanted to wake from a dream. "They were finishing the job," my father added in a low, tight voice. "In broad daylight."

My mother waited for him to say something else. When he didn't, she looked past him at

Samuel. My brother pushed himself off the door frame. "There were hundreds of the tea chests—some of them didn't sink." His eyes were staring at midair, like he could picture it all too clearly. "The boatmen were beating at them with poles and oars, making sure the tea was ruined."

"We need more soldiers," my mother said firmly. "The king will send them."

My father exhaled. "But soldiers fight, my dear. That is all they know how to do. More soldiers will mean more fighting." He nudged his wig. "Not that I see any other solution at this point. The king won't let this go unpunished."

"*Will* the king send more men?" my mother asked.

My father shrugged. "Probably. What else can he do? If he lets this act of madness stand unchallenged, the world will laugh at him and the rebels will be bolder the next time and the next, until there are no laws."

"He might lift the restrictions on tea imports," Samuel said quietly.

My father turned to look at him.

Sam lifted his chin. "Maybe His Majesty will stop imposing taxes without giving us our own representative in Parliament."

I could not see my father's face, but I saw his shoulders rise. "I know this all seems heroic to you, Samuel. Exciting. But you are a boy, and you don't yet understand the ways of the world. Kings do not have endless patience, and they are not frightened by half-wits dressed up in Indian costumes chopping open tea chests with hatchets."

I caught my breath and could not find my voice, but my mother asked the question I wanted to ask.

"What are you talking about?"

My father let out a weary breath. "They dressed up as Indians. Heaven only knows why. They had feathers in their hair, buckskin shirts. I suppose they didn't want their neighbors to recognize them."

"Cowards as well as ruffians, then." My mother closed her mouth firmly.

"Take extra care," my father said, looking at my mother, then me, then Samuel. "Stay away from the docks for a while, make sure you get home before evening falls if you have errands."

My mother covered her heart with one hand. "Surely you don't think that anyone will do us harm?"

My father shook his head. "I can't be sure of anything just now, Charity."

I winced. He almost never used my mother's first name in front of Samuel and me. And he sounded so tired. Through all the disagreements and problems that the colonials had had with King George, my father had never been concerned enough to warn us this way. That meant that now he was afraid, too, and that scared me more than anything. If there were cannonballs shot into the city, if we had to flee, where would we go? And what would happen to Lily?

"I am going out to the stable," Samuel said into the silence that had fallen over the kitchen. "I want to check my gelding."

"I want to go, too," I said, hoping my mother would let me if I caught her off guard. But it did not work.

"Silence, stay to help with breakfast, please." She looked over my head at my brother. "Tap on Prissy's door on your way, will you?"

"I will," Samuel said, then he was gone. My father followed him out, and I could hear them talking in low voices as they went up the hall.

"Start the day's fire," my mother said. "Then put on the kettle."

"Couldn't Prissy do this while I—"

"Silence!" my mother scolded, and I could see how tight her mouth was. "There is no real reason for you to go out to the stables. Is there?"

I wanted to shout that yes, there was a reason. I had to ask Sam what to do. If father knew that Elijah had helped dump the king's tea into the harbor, he would sell his contract to the first bidder and Elijah would be gone from us forever—and who knew what kind of master he would end up with? I didn't want that. But I didn't want him riding Lily without permission, either. Not ever again.

"Start the fire," my mother repeated. She shivered, and I noticed for the first time how cold I was.

Hands numb and thoughts spinning, I used the little iron rake to push back the gray ashes and expose the smoldering coals beneath. They were bright-hot, so I didn't have to use the rope straw to get a flame, I just went through the wood box and found the smallest kindling I could, then blew on the coals until it caught.

"Silence?" I turned when my mother said my name. She looked so serious, so worried, that it frightened me even more. "Perhaps we should go back to England and—"

"Oh, Mother, you don't mean that," Samuel said from the doorway, and we both jumped, startled. He apologized. But then he looked at my mother intently. "Silence and I have never seen England. This is our home—and all this will settle itself soon."

My mother nodded. "Of course you would be reluctant," she said. "But if your father decides that it is best, we will go."

I waited for Samuel to say something more, but he did not. He only lowered his head and asked when breakfast might be ready.

"Half an hour," Mother said. "Did you waken Prissy?"

Samuel nodded.

"Will you tell your father that I would like to discuss something with him when he can take the time?" Samuel nodded again. Once Mother turned back to the hearth, he shot me an odd, intense look that I couldn't make sense out of, then he was gone.

I felt very strange all the rest of that day. There was no further chance to talk to Elijah, or Samuel. I fell asleep thinking this: I would never tell Elijah's secret to anyone for one simple reason. He had never told mine, though I was sure he had heard me come into the barn to see Lily at least one or twice—perhaps dozens of times. But he would have to give me his word that he would never take Lily out of her stall without asking me again, whether or not Father had told him to. Galloping her at night was reckless; a leg injury could kill her. I could not let that happen.

CHAPTER EIGHT

❧ ❧ ❧

*T*he next morning, I managed to run out to the barn when Mother sent me to wake Prissy. Elijah was filling the hayricks, and the dust in the air made me sneeze as I came in. He turned, startled. When he saw it was me, he lowered his head. "Good morning, Miss Silence."

"Is Simon close by?" I whispered.

He shook his head. "He's walking Sam's gelding."

"I'm not going to tell anyone," I said, glancing over my shoulder toward the house path. "But you have to give me your word."

He lifted his eyes. "My word on what?"

"That you will never take Lily anywhere without asking me. Even if my father tells you to ride her, you have to come to me first."

"You love that mare," he said quietly.

I nodded. "I do. If she broke a leg galloping in the dark, or if someone else stole her and I never saw her again, or . . ." I meant to go on. I wanted him to understand. But instead of sounding stern and angry, I started to cry. He waited politely while I sniffled and wiped my eyes and recovered myself. "If you ever do it again, I will have to tell my—"

"Please, Miss Silence," he interrupted me. "I give you my word." His eyes were shiny, and he met my stare and returned it, hard. He meant what he was saying.

I wanted to hug him, but of course I did not. Instead, I ran to Lily's stall and spoke to her for a moment before I started back to the house. I was still worried about the king and the rebels and my mother wanting to go back to England—but knowing that I had Elijah's word eased my heart a little: a promise was better than nothing. But I would be watching him.

The next week passed quickly, and Christmas morning dawned. Our usual observance was as scant as anyone's. The schools were open, as always, as were all the shops and merchant yards. Most stay at home and do their usual work, of course; no one I know disobeys the old decree—and my mother was raised a Puritan, after all. My family would be the last to defy custom and celebrate Christmas.

Still, to please my father, Mother usually made a pudding to serve with supper. I often forgot that it *was* Christmastide until I saw the pudding. On Christmas Day only one special thing happened. Mother and Prissy and I began to reduce a half year's collection of cooking fat into the thick, sharp-smelling mixture that would receive the lye when my mother decided to make soap.

The next day went to housework, too—as nearly all my days did—and the next and the next. Mother didn't want me to ride anywhere now, not even with the boys. I knew she was worried about the rough men and the angry boys in the streets and just wanted me safe. But it was awful. I went out to the barn sometimes, after dark, when Simon and Elijah were asleep. If I saw Elijah in the daytime, he was as polite and kind as he always had been. It was as though the night I had surprised him brushing out Lily's wet coat had never happened.

People had begun calling December 16's events the "Boston Tea Party," which infuriated my father and my mother—it had not been a party, nor any other kind of celebration. It had made light of breaking the law, of stealing and defying a royal decree. And Samuel said that everyone expected the king to send soldiers. That scared me. I had not forgotten what my father had told my mother. Soldiers fight. That is what they know how to do.

Days later, Samuel heard something in the markets that he repeated to me. We were not alone in our troubles. Other colonies up and down the seaboard had found their own ways to prevent the tea from being unloaded and sold. He said everyone was waiting to see how angry the king would be. It was terrible, just waiting, but it was all any of us could do.

I listened to Mother's concerns every day as we worked. I hated it, because it scared me, but I did not know how to make her stop. She was frightened, and angry. She was certain that the ruffians were going to ruin the colonies and make them lawless, unfit for proper people. She seemed just as certain that we should pack up and go back to England at the first sign of good weather, that the Boston Tea Party had been proof there could never be any kind of responsible civilization here. I could tell Father thought she was scaring me more than was needed. But he didn't argue with her, at least not in my hearing. No one argued with her. Not even Sam.

Then, one morning, when she was lamenting that she and Father had ever come to the colonies at all, Samuel said something that made me pause in my scrubbing and listen. "Mother, in England no one can ever rise above his father's place in life."

Mother straightened. "Your father is a respected man, and he—"

"I am fortunate, Mother," Samuel interrupted quietly. "But many are not. Prissy would scrub other people's floors for all her days on this earth in England. Here she can hope for better once Father frees her. Elijah will be twenty when he finishes his contract. He is very good with horses. If I had a stables here, he could be my trainer or even my business partner. In England, he wouldn't ever have a chance to—"

"That has nothing to do with us," my mother cut him off. "Your father will treat Prissy and Elijah fairly, of course, whether we stay or go. But he will make decisions that protect his own family, not a slave or some indentured boy of uncertain birth, no matter how fond he is of both of them."

I was watching Samuel's face as my mother spoke. His eyes darkened—and I realized something. In the same way that Prissy was like an older sister to me, Elijah was like a brother to him. They had grown up together. And I knew, even if my mother did not, that Sam had probably thought about having Elijah as a partner one day, or he would never have said it.

And for the first time in my life, I understood something else. My mother didn't regard either Prissy or Elijah—or even Simon—as anything more than servants. She treated them fairly because it bespoke of her own good character, not because she loved any of them. Knowing that made me sad. It also made me determined to do what I could to help Prissy from that moment to the grave.

"Mother, things will be fine here by and by," Samuel was saying. "The king will have to see that—"

"Enough, Samuel!" my mother scolded, with the usual warm tone beneath the scolding. "Of course you are right. Your father and the rest of the king's loyal men will find a way through this."

My brother nodded obediently, and they spoke of other things for a few minutes, then he left. I wondered if Samuel would feel differently about Elijah as a business partner if he knew what I knew—that Elijah had been involved in destroying the tea, bringing the king's anger and danger to all of us.

And then I had to wonder, all over again, if I should tell, in spite of what I had said to Elijah. I ended up deciding, once more, not to. If the king sent more men, and I had overheard my father telling Anne's father that he almost certainly would, there would be fighting. And then Elijah would regret what he had done, I was sure. He had always been a gentle boy who meant no harm. Probably the hotheaded men on the docks had talked him into it, preferring that an innocent indentured boy take the risk of being caught—instead of themselves.

🎗 🎗 🎗

After a few weeks had passed, Mother stopped talking about going back to England. Samuel continued to ask questions at the supper table now and then, and Father answered him, usually anyway. So Mother and I and Prissy—who was serving and listening—knew more than we ever had before about the king and his laws and other affairs usually kept among the men.

The more time that went by, the less I worried. Maybe Samuel would be right. Maybe the king would remove the tea tax the way he had given up on some of his other taxes. Maybe he would just forget that he had colonies. I began to hope.

Best of all, Samuel eventually talked Mother into letting me ride with him, promising he would keep me close and away from danger. His gelding's stone bruise was nearly healed and it was time to give him more exercise.

I was so happy to be riding Lily! We began with a long clip-clopping walk down Marlborough Street and past the Old North Meeting House. It was icy-chilly, the kind of cold that made me long for spring. But there was only a little snow on the ground, mostly in patches where the wind had drifted it. On the way home, Samuel led the way to the Common. Lily pranced, hoping for a race. I reined her in, knowing Sam's gelding couldn't—not yet.

"Go ahead and canter," Samuel said. "Have a nice run. Just keep me in sight."

I nodded and leaned forward, easing the pressure on the reins. Lily rose into her lovely, rocking canter, and I held her to it long enough to be sure there were no children playing or men duck hunting along the marsh. Then I let her out. As we pounded along a path that led to a stand of trees, I heard a shout and turned to glance at three boys riding side by side. They were grinning at me. One waved. I blushed and let Lily go flat out just long enough to get out of their sight. Then I reined her into a long half circle and started back, bearing to the left far enough that I wouldn't see the boys again.

"It's a shame *you* aren't a boy," Sam said when I told him what had happened.

I laughed. "Why?"

"You ride so well. And you would love owning a stables, I think."

The idea made me get gooseflesh. Own a stables? Raise horses of my own? Oh, how I wished it were possible. I was quiet so long, thinking about it, that Sam leaned out of his saddle to touch my arm. "Come back from the clouds, little sister. What are you thinking such deep thoughts about?"

I turned to look at him, but I didn't answer for a moment. I was embarrassed to tell the truth, and I didn't want to lie. "I have always thought I would try hard to find a husband who let me ride every day," I finally said. "One who wouldn't mind if I spent half my day in the barn." I waited for him to laugh, but he didn't.

"Do you know who Mercy Otis Warren is?" he asked me after a moment.

I shook my head.

"She writes with the most astounding wit and clarity about all that is going on." He leaned toward me. "There are rumors she writes some of the pamphlets and broadsides—even some of the speeches that are given in the meeting houses."

I blinked, amazed. I waited for him to laugh, or cross his eyes or something so that I would know he was teasing, making a joke of what I had said. But he didn't. "Bring me something she's written, Samuel. Please?"

He nodded. "Will you keep it hidden? Father will be furious if he sees it. And Mother."

I promised. And all the way home I kept thinking about what Samuel had said about Elijah being his partner in a horse farm. Was it so very much stranger to think of a woman having a horse farm? I imagined tending to my brood mares, gentling the colts every spring the way I had worked with Lily.

I thought about it so much that I couldn't sleep that night. Sometime after midnight, I got up, dressed, and opened my shutters. There was a big moon lighting the path to the stables. I made sure the house was silent, then I ran out to the barn, intending to check on Lily, and maybe tell her about the horse farm—I couldn't think of anyone else who would listen. But the moment I eased open the wide barn door, all my day-dreaming faded like steam in a warm kitchen. Elijah was brushing Lily, the lantern low so he wouldn't wake Simon, and her coat was wet with sweat again.

CHAPTER NINE

❧ ❧ ❧

I was so angry that I didn't speak a single word to Elijah. He had *promised* me. He had given his solemn word, and he had broken it. Our eyes met for an instant, then I opened the stall gate and walked Lily in a circle to make sure she was unhurt. Then I left the barn running, clambering over my windowsill and going straight down the hall. I woke my parents without once considering how I was going to explain myself.

They sat up in bed, their backs against their headboard. It was chilly enough that our breath showed in the light of the candle my mother lit, then set on her nightstand. My father found his pocket watch and frowned at it, then laid it down. I knew I should be thinking about how to tell them, what to say, but I was too angry to think, to do anything but tell the simple truth.

"And you just go out to the barn?" my mother interrupted. "Without telling anyone? How often?"

I shook my head. I really didn't know. I had never kept track. "Just . . . sometimes," I said weakly, and I saw her face harden in the candlelight.

"You will not ride until I give you my permission. Is that clear?"

I was shivering now that the heat of my anger had subsided, and I pulled my shawl closer. "You can punish me if you like," I told her. "But Elijah can't keep risking hurting Lily on these night rides."

"Where in the world is he going?" my father asked. I pulled in a breath, not wanting to tell the whole, complicated truth about how I had found the Indian costume and what I suspected and—

"Is there some girl whom he—" my father began, interrupting my frantic thoughts. Then he looked past me, toward the chamber door. Samuel was standing there in his nightshirt and cap, rubbing his eyes. "What is this about? Is everyone all right?"

My father explained. Then he cleared his throat. "Does Elijah have a girl he might be visiting to take walks in the moonlight?"

Samuel looked confused, like all this was too much for him to take in. He finally shook his head, then hesitated. "You know, there is a girl I have noticed smiling at him when we ride past the market on the way to the Common. She's pretty."

My father sighed. Then he yawned. "To bed, both of you. I will take care of all this in the morning."

I stood staring at him. "But we have to make sure that—"

"Elijah is growing up, Silence," he said wearily. "I will make it plain to him that he cannot forget for an instant who owns the mare—and his indenture contract."

I took a breath. "But this can't wait until—"

"Morning is only about three hours away, Silence," he said. "Go to bed."

Samuel took a step forward and hooked his arm through mine. He guided me into the hallway and closed the chamber door behind us. "I will have a talk with him, too," Samuel said, reaching out to tuck my hair behind my ear. I slapped at his hand. He looked shocked, then apologetic. "I didn't mean to startle you."

I wasn't sure what I would say if I opened my mouth, so I pressed my lips together and walked fast up the hallway. I wasn't startled, I was furious. Mother and Father weren't capable of being truly angry with him. But I knew it was different with me. Elijah would be scolded roundly, too, of that I had no doubt. But I would probably end up in as much trouble as he did—and that seemed ridiculous to me. I had done *nothing* that would harm anyone or anything. And he had.

Samuel didn't call after me, and I didn't look back at him. I went straight into my room, undressed, and got into bed. It took half of eternity for me to go to sleep, but once I had, I stayed asleep until the sun was up. And it was a shout of pain that wakened me.

My eyes flew open, and my heart thudded inside my chest. I sat up, listening, telling myself that it had been a bad dream—and then the cry came again—softer, from the barn. I leaped out of bed and dressed in a trice, then ran. As I got close, I heard a low moan. I stumbled to a stop, staring through the big double doors. My father was holding Simon's carriage whip. But he wasn't using it to convince a horse to do something it didn't want to do. He was using it on Elijah.

Elijah was standing with his bare back to my father, his arms stretched up to grip the top rail of Lily's stall gate. There was an ugly crisscrossing of long red welts on his back. My father raised his hand once more, and Elijah grunted when the long knotted strands of rawhide hit his already bloody skin. I winced and cried out louder than he had.

My father turned and saw me. He coiled the whip, frowning. "Did you tell your mother you were coming out here?"

I shook my head, feeling sick. "She wasn't up yet," I managed to whisper. "And I heard . . ." I waved one hand toward Elijah. This close, I could see that his knees were shaking. His whole body was trembling.

"Don't. Please don't. Just don't whip him anymore," I whispered to my father, wishing I had never told my parents. I should have *thought.* I should have confided in Samuel, and he would have done something, but not . . . *this.*

"Go back inside," my father said sharply.

"Father, please, don't—"

He leaned close, his voice tight, his words separated by tiny pauses. "Go. Back. Inside."

I turned, stumbling once, my feet and legs weighted with guilt. I pulled open the door to the house and nearly ran into my brother. I grabbed his coat sleeve. "Did Father tell you? Did you know?" I hissed at him.

"Know what?"

"Father is *whipping* Elijah," I managed, my throat tight and painful, then I tried to push past him.

He caught my wrist and jerked me around to face him. "What? Now?"

I nodded, and he was off at a run without another word to me. I stood shivering, listening to the sound of his footfalls get softer when he rounded the corner of the house. Father might listen to Samuel. I hoped he would.

I found my mother in the kitchen starting the fire. "Sit down," she said, as though this was any normal morning on any normal day. Then she added this: "I don't know what you have been thinking, Silence. Eavesdropping. Going out windows at night." She paused. "Your father will set Elijah straight," she added. "But that mare is a constant worry for me. You lose your common sense when it comes to that animal."

I had no idea what to say. My heart was breaking, for Elijah, for Lily, for myself. I hurt too much to cry. I could only sit still and wait for my mother to tell me what to do. "Clean the hearth," she said. "I will go wake Prissy." She looked sad and pale. I waited for her to scold me, or give me extra chores. But she didn't. I think Father's whipping Elijah was as much anger as she could stand.

I thought that terrible day would never pass, but it did. Slowly. Miserably. After supper, when at last, at last, it was finally over, I went to my room. I stole out to the barn after dark. I knew it was foolish. I knew that if my mother happened to get up and notice, I would be punished terribly. But I couldn't stand the way I felt, and I knew being with Lily would make me hurt a little less.

I cried, leaning against Lily's warm shoulder. I could hear Elijah breathing, louder than usual. And once, when he turned on his cot, I heard him make a little sound of pain without waking. Lily lifted her head and stamped one forehoof.

I stopped crying. It had to have taken him a long time to get to sleep, his poor back welted and bloody; the last thing I meant to do was wake him. I found myself whispering to Lily, apologizing to her for hurting her friend—because Elijah was truly that. He took very good care of her. My feelings were painfully knotted. I had caused Elijah to be whipped, and I was sorry. But he had taken my Lily and galloped her hard in the darkness, taking a chance with her very life. I was angry and sorrowful, both at once. Not even Lily's warm breath in my hair could truly ease my heart that night.

❧ ❧ ❧

As the cold gray days dragged past, my parents did not speak again about what Elijah had done—or what Father had done to him. I thought about it every day—it had changed me somehow, deep in my heart. Samuel was somber, answering Father in short, clipped sentences. I don't think Father noticed; he was preoccupied with the growing talk of rebellion in the city. Or, if he did notice, I am sure he thought Samuel would one day see the necessity of what he had done.

I never would.

Never.

And I was sure Elijah wouldn't either.

Maybe that was the difference between growing up in England and growing up here, in the colonies. Here, there were fewer differences between us, between servants and masters. We were new in this land, where only the Indians had been before us. We were building this place, not just living in it, and we all had dreams of a bright new future. I knew what I wanted now that Samuel had put it in my mind. I just didn't know how I might get it.

"I am so sorry," I told Elijah when I finally found him alone in the barn one morning. I felt tears seep into my eyes. "I only want Lily to be safe.

I didn't know my father would . . ." and I stopped there because I couldn't bring myself to say the words.

"I understand," he said quietly, and then he would say no more.

🎭 🎭 🎭

As the weather slowly turned and warmed, Boston settled back into the familiar rhythms I had known all of my life—ships coming and going, Mrs. Chester's instructions, Anne and Sarah finding ways to make me laugh when I shouldn't. We were learning to dance now, the more complicated steps that we would need when we had real young men as partners. The idea of going to balls made me uneasy.

I told Prissy, and she smiled and told me that I would be less uneasy once I had done it once or twice, just like with anything else. And she said Samuel would practice dancing with me if I asked him. I hadn't thought of that, and it made me feel a little better. Then I felt silly. If war was coming, dancing wouldn't matter.

After one of our lessons, Anne leaned close to whisper once Mrs. Chester had left the room. "Alain asks after you whenever he sees me," she said.

I felt my cheeks flush, and it made me angry. But instead of teasing me, Anne's face was serious. "His father is supporting the rebels, I think, Silence. Poor Alain. People are finding out; he might not be invited to any of the spring balls."

I felt my stomach tighten. How could there be balls? Now? With everyone treading lightly, watching the harbor, wondering if the king's warships were on their way? "My father says we will all know soon whether or not the king is going to take drastic measures," I breathed, in case Mrs. Chester was listening from the hall. "The weather is good enough for the king's ships to sail."

Sarah's answer was just as quiet. "My father won't speak about any of it anymore. He thinks the rebels have to be defeated, with whatever force, or the colonies will collapse into disorder."

I nodded. "My father says much the same. And he isn't talking about it now either, not as much. He—" I stopped midsentence because I heard Mrs. Chester's heavy step as she came back up the hall. I glanced out the window and blinked, not believing my own eyes for an instant. My brother was waiting, riding his gelding, and leading my Lily.

Lily!

As soon as Mrs. Chester dismissed us, I left in an excited rush and ran down the walk. Samuel laughed at how excited I was. "Does Mother know?"

He shook his head. "She's off to a spinning day, and Simon has driven her in the carriage, so there is no one home to tell the tale. Father is at meetings with his financial partners that he said would last until supper most likely. So it seemed the perfect day for a ride."

I flew into his arms, and he laughed as he helped me into my sidesaddle. I thanked him again and again as he mounted. Then we set off. Lily tossed her head and tried to break into a canter. I reined her in. Most of the way back through Boston, she was excited, prancing sideways on the cobblestones. It was heavenly to be riding her when I had been so sure I could not for a long time. I started to thank Samuel once more, and he smiled and bade me stop. Lily slowly settled down as we went, cantering once or twice across open fields, then slowing again when we came back onto the street.

The first glimmer of spring green was showing in the matted grass on the Common. Lily and I took a careful gallop on the slick, sodden ground, staying away from the dirty drifts of snow along the marsh. The rhythm of her stride soothed my heart the way it always did. My hair flew out behind us and for a while, I didn't worry about anything.

My brother cantered his gelding in a wide, easy circle until Lily and I had galloped ourselves breathless. It was glorious. My hair was loose, and the wind of our passage lifted it and Lily's mane like flags. When we finally came trotting back, I pulled Lily around and she cantered beside Sam's gelding. "He's not favoring the bruised hoof anymore," I said, listening to the even cadence of his hooves.

Samuel smiled. "Not a bit. He's sound. One day soon, we'll have another race."

I smiled. "I can't wait." I wanted to stay on Lily until it was too dark to see, but I knew we had to get home before our parents. So I finally turned Lily toward Frog Lane, and Samuel followed. Elijah unsaddled the horses and I rubbed Lily down quickly, hating to leave her. Then Samuel took me by the hand and led me toward the house. "Are you sure that Elijah won't tell Mother I've been riding? Promise?" I whispered.

He slowed to look into my face. "On my life."

"But he took Lily and—"

"Not now," Samuel said. "Not on the heels of such a fine day of riding."

I nodded, and we went inside.

Mother came home first. I was starting supper with Prissy when my father came home, bringing a guest. I overheard them talking about the price of molasses and linen cloth as they stood before the kitchen hearth long enough to get warm, then they went to the parlor and closed the door. It had been the kind of conversation I had listened to all of my life. My father was always buying and selling cargos. And when Mother came home, she talked about her spinning day, nothing more. She had stopped talking about going back to England, and I was grateful. There was no war talk from anyone that evening. It was as though our lives might just go on, as they always had.

And then, one day not long after that, an English warship sailed into our harbor, and no one had to wonder any longer how angry the ruined tea would make the king. The news spread fast. Parliament was passing new laws concerning the colonies. My father left a broadside on the parlor table, and when Mother had me oil the chair rails, I read it. The king's Parliament had passed laws they were calling the Coercive Acts. The first one seemed fair enough to my father.

"This should satisfy any reasonable man," he said at supper one night, waving the broadside I had read.

"But they are closing the harbor," Samuel said. "That means colonial ships can't bring in anything at all until—"

"Until the tea is paid for and the customs officers who were treated roughly receive payments for their injuries. Does this seem unreasonable to you?"

Samuel shook his head and didn't speak.

"And the port will be closed for only a short time, I am sure," Father said firmly. "Then men of reason will prevail."

Samuel took a drink of his cider, then set down the mug. "But none of this solves the real problem."

My father shook his head. "Again, I will say it, Sam. You are a boy. But even you cannot expect the king simply to forget what the Tea Party cost the East India Company, nor his officials' injuries, nor can he "

"Samuel Adams and others say we should have a representative in Parliament," Sam interrupted. "That seems reasonable, too."

My father had been about to put a bit of chicken stew in his mouth. The spoon stopped halfway, and he looked at Sam. "You are not going to meetings to hear these fools speak, are you?"

Sam hesitated. "Others do," he said, waving one hand vaguely. "People talk about what they say. And there are the broadsides and Mrs. Warren's plays."

Father nodded. "Don't be swayed by any of it. We will have a representative in Parliament one day, but I won't live to see it, and you might not, either. We are colonists, Samuel, not a sovereign country. We need the king and his army to protect us and to keep order. And for those services, we will pay something, one way or another."

Sam nodded, then went quiet and ate without talking or looking up until his bowl was emptied. That night, he tapped lightly on my door. He handed me a pamphlet, printed on cheap paper. It was a play written by Mercy Otis Warren. "Don't let Mother or Father see it, and when you are finished, burn it."

I blinked. "Why?"

"Because the play makes fun of what is happening now. She's writing about the colonies, even though she doesn't say so."

I read the play slowly. It began in a place Mrs. Warren called Servia:

Brutus:
Is this the once famed mistress of the north
The sweet retreat of freedom? Dearly purchased
A clime matured with blood; from whose rich soil,
Has sprung a glorious harvest. Oh! my friend . . .
The change how drear! The sullen ghost of bondage
Stalks full in view—

I wasn't sure I understood it all, but one thing was clear. Mercy Otis Warren thought kings should be questioned and freedom held very dear. I wondered if my father would read it. Mrs. Warren spoke about things women were supposed to leave to men.

I stole into the kitchen and blew on the hearth coals to make the flame rise quickly, then burned the play. Then I slipped out to the barn to talk to Lily for a moment before I undressed for bed.

Simon and Elijah were already asleep, both of them snoring. I rubbed Lily's face and ears, then leaned close to whisper what I hadn't dared say, even to myself. "Lily," I breathed. "I think Elijah is talking to Samuel about the rebels. Maybe Sam knows that Elijah helped dump the tea in the harbor and is keeping it secret." I sighed, feeling helpless. "Father will never forgive either one of them if he finds out."

CHAPTER TEN

❦ ❦ ❦

April was fine and warm, and May was warmer still. My mother's tansy and campanula came up and bloomed in the window boxes—and she planted her garden. But the harbor was still closed, and men all over the city were angry and worried. I know my father was. Things had gotten worse, not better. Mother insisted we stay off the streets. She was afraid of being caught in the middle of a fight if one broke out. My lessons with Mrs. Chester were less regular, then stopped altogether when she left Boston with her family. I missed Anne and Sarah sorely.

Every day I looked for a chance to ask my father if I could ride Lily, but when I saw the strain in his face, I did not want to cause him more trouble, knowing that my mother would argue against it.

So I visited the barn at night and talked to her endlessly, sometimes sitting astride her back, bent forward over her withers, my arms around her neck. She was strong and fit. Elijah led her along when he exercised the other horses. In the night-quiet barn, with Lily's warm breath on my hands and in my hair, I could stop worrying. It was the only place I *wasn't* half afraid.

"They are going to bring us to war," my father said at the supper table one night. "How can they refuse to pay reasonable damages?"

I looked at Samuel as Father said it, but he was eating, his head down. Father sighed. "I don't know how much longer we can all stand this."

I thought for a moment he was talking about us, his family; then I realized that he meant everyone in the colony. I knew that my father's ships were docked and that all but a few of the sailors had disappeared, looking for work in the countryside. I knew we were poorer by the day because of it and that we weren't the only ones. When I went with Mother on errands, there were more and more ragged men on the street, more signs advertising the barter of work for a meal.

Our spirits were down, too. Prissy was singing less—probably because my mother was so upset over everything, so easily irritated, that we were all being careful around her. Samuel walked through the house silent and tense much of the time. Mother asked me if I knew if he was troubled by anything beyond what everyone was worrying over. I told her I did not—and was glad when she didn't press me for a guess. Sam had completely stopped asking Father questions at supper—I was pretty sure that he had stopped talking to my father about the king and his taxes altogether. If my father noticed, he said nothing. He was quieter, too, and he looked tired. His meetings in the parlor had dwindled—maybe all the men had little left to say to one another.

Mother and I went out in the carriage only in the middle of the day, and, even then, I could see that she was nervous. More than once, we turned a corner to find a crowd of men standing before a fence or a wide-trunked tree, reading a broadside that had been nailed up. They were always standing in a loose half circle, more or less orderly, but if someone was reading aloud, he was interrupted by rounds of jeering, or huzzahs.

I listened hard, catching bits and pieces of what was being said. They talked about natural rights that belonged to all men. I had never heard of such a thing. I asked Sam if he had. He shook his head. "I don't think anyone ever has." And then he left me before I could ask him more questions. I wanted to know if they meant indentured boys, too, and slaves, and every man who was too poor to pay taxes or own land. Did they mean *women*?

One morning I asked my father how much longer he thought it would take for the colonies to reach an agreement with the king.

"I wish I knew the answer to that," he said quietly. "Tell your mother I will be back for dinner at noon."

Watching him stride toward the door, I wished, desperately, that some solution could be found that would satisfy all of the men, the English and the colonials—and the king, too. It did not seem likely.

Just past mid-May, another law was given out, and even my father was upset by the new one. At supper he laid down his fork and sighed. Mother and I leaned forward, and I saw Prissy pause and turn to listen. "The assembly is to be ended," he said bitterly. "All the good men we elected to advise and lead us will be replaced by men the king's governor appoints. No town meetings are allowed without his permission, and we can no longer elect juries." He paused to take in a long breath. "The harbor is still closed, and I don't doubt more troops are coming." He shook his head. "We are under control of the king. And that is the start and the end of it. I did not think he would go this far."

"Oh, dear," my mother breathed. "Will it work? Will the ruffians give up their nonsense?"

He shook his head. "I don't know. I think not."

I watched in my usually silent way—to keep anyone from remembering they shouldn't talk in front of me about such weighty things. I looked at Samuel, but he had his head down, fiddling with the scant bit of fried fish on his plate. Suppers had become simpler and smaller than I ever remembered them. We never spoke of it. But I knew the reason. Day and night, the king's warships were prowling along the coast, ready to attack any ship that tried to sail into or out of Boston Harbor.

There was little to buy and scant money to buy it. The harbor was closed, *still*. Father made no money from his ships now. Supplies were short in the whole of the New England colonies. Farmers from the countryside were selling whatever they could grow, and all of Boston's wives were planting little gardens and spinning their own wool. My mother, of course, thought it was about time they did. Her garden was up and blooming as soon as the weather warmed.

"Perhaps we should think again about going back to England," she said very quietly one evening.

Father made a vague gesture with one hand, a vexed look on his face. "It is my hope that the colonists will neither fight, nor run. Either will spell the doom of the colonies." He drew in a long breath. "There is little use in spoiling every meal talking about all this," he said, his eyes meeting mine, then Mother's, then Samuel's. After that, none of us said much at supper.

Often, I lay in my bed in the dark with my eyes wide open, worrying. Sometimes I got up to go see Lily, and that usually helped tame my fears. But sometimes even Lily couldn't comfort me. One night I lay awake until dawn. I felt like we were all standing in the shadow of a heavy-limbed tree and the wind was rising.

It was a grim and painful time, even though the spring was unfolding into full summer with each day that passed. Mother and I were in the carriage one morning when a crowd of men came running down the street, shouting and cursing. Behind them rode four English soldiers, demanding that they stop. Simon reined in the mares, and the ragged crowd of men passed on both sides of the carriage. One man jumped into the coach with us. "Maybe these fine, king-loving Tory ladies will share their—"

"Begone!" Simon shouted, turning as he rose, the buggy whip raised in his right hand. The man laughed and jumped back into the street, sprinting to catch up with his companions. I realized I was holding my breath and let it out. Mother's face was white.

"Thank you, Simon," she said. "Take us home now, please."

We sat in silence as Simon urged the mares into a smart trot and turned at the next corner, then the next, heading home. I could hear shouts somewhere off toward the bay and wondered what had happened.

"I hate these lazy, do-nothing troublemakers," my mother said quietly.

I didn't answer. She was wrong. I had started noticing how the men were dressed: their vests, their wigs. Most were not wealthy men—some of them might even be indentured, like Elijah. Many were probably apprentices in some trade shop, farm boys come to town to learn how to blacksmith or build beds or work silver. But they were not lazy. They had the hands and arms of men who worked hard at something. And, as

I had noticed all along, there were more than a few with soft leather shoes and silver buttons on their shirts.

"Until this sorts itself out, I will send Simon to do what needs doing," my mother said that evening at supper. "We shall stay at home until it is safe for decent women and girls in these streets."

And she meant it. For the next two weeks, we went nowhere at all. She gave me strict orders to speak to no one I did not know. And if I saw a band of ruffians coming near the house, I was to run to tell her immediately. It was awful. No one slept soundly; we were always listening, always watching. We were all waiting for the worst.

One evening at supper, Father told us that the British troops were making arrests in the streets, breaking up meetings in taverns and shops, trying to apprehend the worst of the rebels. "Good," Mother said. "I knew more soldiers was the answer."

My father shrugged. "I am not so sure of that. We are all used to being able to argue our own affairs here. My own guests and I do much the same thing."

My mother shook her head. "Nonsense. It isn't the same at all."

Father laid down his knife. "I wonder some-times."

Mother clucked like a disapproving hen, but his words made me think. It *wasn't* different in most ways; both sides were just groups of men gathering to talk about decisions that had to be made for the colonies. Some had fancy parlors to meet in. Others did not. I looked up and saw Samuel staring off at the wall, pretending not to notice Mother trying to catch his eye.

In June, a law called the Quartering Act was approved by the English Parliament. What it meant was this: King George had run out of places to house all the soldiers he had sent to Boston. So he had passed a law saying that they could be assigned to live in any empty house or shed or anywhere at all, including anyone's house—our house. And that is what happened.

One evening, my father told us that he had been notified that our home was to quarter three British soldiers—one officer and his two aids. And the next morning, they pounded on our front door. I looked at the hall clock. It wasn't much past six o'clock. Mother and Prissy and I were up. My father and Samuel were not.

Mother woke Father, and he dressed and came down the hall to receive the soldiers.

I heard him greet them and welcome them, explaining that their horses would be kept in one of the fields. The weather was warm, and there were no empty stalls in our barn. Then his voice dropped a little, and I couldn't make out what he was saying. They walked down the hall, and I caught a glimpse as they passed the kitchen door. The aids were both small, wiry young men, and the officer, with his fancy coat and black boots, was older and much taller. They all wore the familiar red coats and sword scabbards I had often seen on the streets of Boston—but it was odd to see them here, in our hallway.

"It is nothing more than plain fare nowadays," I heard my father say. "But you are welcome to take your meals with us."

I didn't hear any of them answer him. The sound of their heavy boots on the stairs made me wince. How odd, that there would be soldiers sleeping upstairs where my mother had planned to have her many children sleeping.

"Silence!" my mother whispered.

I turned, afraid I was going to be in trouble for eavesdropping again. But that wasn't her concern.

"Run tell Prissy they have arrived. I sent her out to get more blankets, but she can bring them here, and I will have Simon take them upstairs later."

I nodded, glad for the chance to do something. I was nervous as a stray cat. This wasn't the first time we'd had strangers in our house. Father had guests sometimes. One of his captains had come from England to Boston, then, after resting from the voyage for a fortnight with us, rode overland to his home in Virginia. But this was different. We had been *ordered* to let these soldiers into our home. It felt wrong.

I went out the front door and followed the path to the side yard, then to the back of the house. I glanced at my own bedroom window as I passed it. The shutters were closed tightly. No one would ever guess how many times I had crawled over the sill on my way to the barn. I found Prissy in the storage shed built onto the backside of the servants' quarters.

"They're here," I told her.

She nodded, her face composed. If she felt one way or another about the soldiers being here, she gave no sign.

"Mother says to bring the blankets in to her, and she will have Simon carry them . . ." I trailed off because I realized she had the blankets in her arms. "I can take them in," I said, reaching out.

She nodded and handed them to me, still not saying a word. And then I realized that her lips were pressed together and that, as I had walked up, she had not been singing. She did not want these house guests—for her own reasons. I could guess what they were. I watched her take a long breath, then she spoke.

"How many?" she asked me.

"Three," I told her.

She nodded. "Everything suits your mother so far?"

"I think so. It's perfectly clean, Prissy. She isn't going to find anything to complain about."

Prissy smiled a little but didn't say anything. Mother had kept us both busy, getting ready. Prissy and I had made sure every single corner and niche of the upstairs was spotless, well aired, rugs beaten clean, sills washed. You would have thought the king himself was coming the way Mother acted.

"I dread to have them here," Prissy said quietly.

I nodded to let her know I felt the same. "They were courteous to Father, at least."

She shook her head, and I could tell that she was annoyed at my quick answer. "War is coming, Silence, and then they will not be courteous."

I had no idea what to say to that, so I said nothing. But as I stood there, staring at her, the blankets clutched against my chest, I felt so uneasy it made my stomach sick.

"Have you seen Samuel?" I asked her.

She nodded. "Rode off hours ago."

"Did he say where?"

She shrugged. "Not to me. But he must have talked to your father before he left."

I sighed, wishing he was home.

"Tell your mother I will be right in," Prissy said. I knew she was reminding me not to waste too much time getting back. If Mother assumed that Prissy was the one who had spent idle time chatting, she would be the one to get the worst scolding.

Supper that night was very strange. The soldiers sat across the wide table from my family. They all wore bright red coats and had dark hats, now removed for politeness' sake. But the tallest man had a much fancier coat, with gold trim at the cuffs and collar. He introduced himself, not the others, who seemed to expect the discourtesy from him. His name was Captain Harvey.

Samuel barely spoke except when good manners demanded that he say something. Mother spoke way too much. She was nervous and apologetic. She was sorry the meat wasn't more abundant in the stew, that the bread was dark, that there were no sweets to begin the meal.

"There is no need to apologize, ma'am," one of the nameless men assured her. His accent was very strange to my ears. He said the word *need* so that it almost rhymed with *braid*.

"No, indeed, ma'am," the other man with a plain red jacket agreed. "This is a long shot better than the slops we had on ship. And looking at a fine lady while I eat is something I never thought—"

"Stop." Captain Harvey leaned forward. "Both of you, be still and eat. Then go back upstairs."

The two men mumbled, "Yes, Cap'n," then lowered their eyes and chewed fast.

I had heard my mother take in a quick breath at the dark-haired soldier's rudeness—and Father had set down his knife and stared—but now she smiled and tipped her head. "Surely, Captain, he meant no harm and—"

"Please, ma'am" he interrupted her. "Their manners are unforgivable. What little their mothers taught them is long since lost in the roughness of their profession."

The two men finished eating faster than hungry dogs might have, then they lifted their heads and sat, waiting for permission from Captain Harvey.

"Go," he said.

They shuffled their feet and stood, then went back into the hallway, headed for the narrow staircase at the far end. I noticed Samuel watching them sharply as they left.

"Captain Harvey," my father said, his face stern, "perhaps for the rest of your stay, you could join us here, and your men could take their meals upstairs?"

A faint smiled flickered on Captain Harvey's face, then disappeared. "You will be glad to know that I agree, sir," he said.

I was looking at my father and saw his reaction. The very idea that Captain Harvey thought his agreement was needed astonished him. This was my father's house.

"I am appreciative of your efforts," Captain Harvey told my mother, licking his fingers instead of using his napkin. I could see my mother trying not to wince. Then, before any more was said, Captain Harvey abruptly took his leave.

"How long will they be here?" Mother whispered after he had left.

"I cannot answer that," my father said. "They will be here until King George no longer requires me to quarter them. I can only hope he will not require Sam or myself to fight beside them."

My mother's eyes were glassy with unshed tears. She stood up.

"Charity," my father said, the hardness gone from his voice. He got up, then reached out to take her hand. I had never seen my parents' affection for each other so plainly. My mother leaned forward so that her forehead rested on his shoulder. They didn't speak, they just stood there. I glanced up to see Sam leaving.

After a moment, I slipped out, too, and ran to the barn. I knew that it was foolish and that if my mother found out I would be sorry. But Simon and Elijah were already asleep, and I stayed only a moment, just long enough to tell Lily that I didn't like Captain Harvey or his men and that I was scared there would soon be fighting. Would my father and Sam have to fight? "I can just feel it," I told her. "Like a storm when the thunder is still far away, but you know it is coming." She lifted her head sharply, as though she understood.

CHAPTER ELEVEN

⚛ ⚛ ⚛

*F*or two weeks, Captain Harvey and his aids came and went, and we never knew where. They kept their saddles and tack in the garden shed. They didn't so much as let my mother know which meals they would attend. I tried not to add to her worries—or my father's. I did my work and stayed out of the way most of the time.

"Silence," my father said to me one evening. "Your mother says you have been a perfect helper lately. If you can spare a little time in the evenings, the mare needs more exercise than Elijah can manage."

My heart leaped. "I can ride Lily?"

He nodded. "Only in the lane, and only once your work is done."

"Thank you," I said, trying not to cry. He patted my head, then my shoulder.

"These are hard times for all of us," he said, and took a deep breath. "And I fear it will get worse. The meetings are getting rougher, more shouting and less reasoning." He paused, and I thought he was going to say something else, but he didn't. I worked so diligently that day that my mother noticed and thanked me. And the instant I could, I ran out to the barn and asked Simon to saddle Lily.

"I will do it," Elijah said, and I turned to look at him.

"Thank you," I said quietly.

When Elijah had Lily's bridle on and the saddle cinched, he stepped back. "Be sure to test it."

I promised I would and met his eyes. "Elijah, I will always be sorry."

He nodded. "Don't let it trouble you anymore, Miss Silence. One day, maybe I can explain."

I nodded. "I hope so." Then he stepped forward and helped me up. I was almost trembling as I rode out of the barn and into the lane. Finally, a chance to ride without hiding it from my parents. I felt my worries easing, and I could tell that Lily was as excited as I was, prancing in a wide circle as I checked the cinch. It was tight.

"Come on, Lily," I whispered to her, leaning forward. She half reared, and I loosened the reins. Lily leaped into a gallop and pounded down the hard-packed road. She resisted the reins when I tried to slow her for the turn, but she made it without slowing, leaning hard to the left. Starting back toward the barn, I could feel the strength of her back legs, every stride still almost a leap forward.

By our second passage, I had Lily more under control, and she slowed to make the turn at the top of the lane. It was then that I noticed Captain Harvey, sitting on his rough-coated gelding, watching. I nodded so that no one could say I had been rude, then made the next turn at the barn, cutting the route in half to avoid seeing him again.

By the time Lily and I were both tired, it was nearly dark. I walked her cool and then hugged her neck hard and told her I loved her before I handed Elijah the reins and started for the house. I felt wonderful—I knew it wouldn't last, but it was so nice that I hoped dinner would be peaceful and that Samuel would talk a little more.

"Supper in two minutes," my mother said when she saw me. I nodded and ran to wash.

Captain Harvey joined us and nodded at me, smiling, as Prissy served the meal. I nodded back, then lowered my eyes. "Your daughter rides better than most our calvary." he said, looking at my father.

Father nodded. "She does indeed."

"I would like to make you an offer on the mare she was riding this evening," he said.

My heart stopped beating. I stared at my charger, fiddling with the food, waiting for my father to tell him Lily wasn't for sale, but he didn't. Astonished, I lifted my eyes and saw Captain Harvey and my father staring at each other, their faces hard and closed. Samuel was watching them, too, his brow creased.

"I will have to think about that," my father said.

Captain Harvey smiled. "Not for too long, I hope. I need a better horse. And I am sure your son has no objection?"

I stared. What was going on? Why would Captain Harvey think Samuel had anything to say about it? I glanced at my brother, but he was staring at his plate. No one spoke for the rest of the meal. I sat stiffly, fighting an impulse to ask my father why in the world he was letting this man think, for even an instant, that he would be able to buy my Lily.

Samuel was the first one to rise and excuse himself. Captain Harvey watched him leave, then shook his head without saying anything. I stared. What was this about? Had my brother argued with the soldiers? My knees were shaking when I asked to be excused a moment later. My mother said no, but my father nodded, so I went out, chasing Samuel down the hall.

"What's the matter with you . . . and father?" I whispered as I caught up. "He can't sell Lily!"

Samuel looked down at me. "Silence, there isn't anything I can say except that I am sorry. I have caused you and our parents more trouble that I ever imagined I would."

"What are you talking about?" I whispered. But he just kissed my forehead, then whispered the same two words against my skin. "I'm sorry."

I slept in fits and starts all night, trying to think what he might have done, what sort of trouble he was in—and what in the world it had to do with Captain Harvey. Only one thing made sense, and it scared me so deeply that I shivered beneath my blankets. I decided I would ask him, straight and true, and demand an answer.

But in the morning, Samuel was gone.

Mother sent Prissy to wake him, and she came back saying his bed had not been slept in. By noon, my mother was beside herself. Father looked angry, and Captain Harvey seemed amused.

"Your son is not sick, I trust. I missed him at breakfast, and he is not eating dinner either?" he said in a mock-polite voice at midday dinner. But he did not wait for an answer. "I suggest that you think about my offer on the mare," he said, rising to leave when he had finished eating. He shouted for his aids from the hallway, and we heard the pounding of their heavy boots as they came down the stairs.

My father went to his study the moment they were gone, and my mother turned to snap orders at Prissy and me. I did my work as quickly as I could, glimpsing the red-coated soldiers riding away through the parlor window. When I could steal a moment, I went out to the barn. I longed to see Lily, and I had to talk to Elijah. Simon was tending to the carriage wheels in the barnyard, coating the oaken spokes with oil to keep the wood from cracking. Perfect.

I walked straight to Lily's stall and scratched her ears and rubbed her forehead. In the stall adjacent, Samuel's gelding whickered. So. Wherever Sam had gone, he had walked. After a long moment, I looked down the barn aisle. Elijah was cleaning the stall at the far end, the pitchfork moving in a steady rhythm.

"Elijah?" I called. He stopped working and looked up, startled. I motioned for him to come closer, and he laid down the pitchfork and walked toward me. I could see the uneasiness in his eyes. I waited until he was close enough to whisper. "Do you know where Sam is?"

"Your father asked me that this morning, Miss Silence," he said quietly. "I told him I didn't."

I leaned closer. "But now I am asking you, Elijah. And I give you my word that I will not tell anyone else." He stared at me, and I knew what he was thinking. He had broken his word to me once, perhaps I would do the same to him. "Just tell me the truth," I begged him. "Where is Samuel?"

"In the countryside, somewhere safe, Miss Silence," he said. "I don't know where, just that he is safe."

I leaned closer. "It was Samuel who rode Lily both those nights . . . and many more, wasn't it?"

Elijah looked at his feet, then at the roof timbers, then at me. He nodded. "Sam was careful with her," he said. "All the galloping was on hard-packed lanes, to get past the patrols."

I exhaled sharply. It was true then. Samuel *was* involved with the rebels—my own brother had helped throw the tea into the harbor. And he was helping bring the colonies closer to war. I stepped back and leaned against Lily's stall gate, trying to get used to the idea. It didn't upset me as much as I thought it should—and I wasn't sure why at first. Then I realized that reading the broadsides and Mrs. Warren's play—and talking to Samuel—had given me an understanding of what the rebels wanted, the freedom they longed for.

"Captain Harvey knows Sam is a rebel, doesn't he?" I asked.

"Captain Harvey arrested Sam a few days ago," Elijah said. "He was reading a broadside posted on a tavern wall with dozens of others. The redcoats called it an illegal meeting by the king's laws." He pulled in a breath and looked around, then back at me. "But Captain Harvey didn't take him to the prisoner house. He just brought him home."

I felt my legs go weak. That explained everything: my father having to consider the offer for Lily; his drawn, gray face. Captain Harvey had told him what Samuel was doing and would now hold it as a threat against us.

"The captain wants to buy Lily," I told Elijah. "And Father said he would consider an offer. Now I know why."

Elijah's face went dark. "He's a bad man, the captain. Sam had every right to read—" he began. Then he realized what he'd said, and he closed his mouth.

I smiled to let him know I already understood his opinions. Then I thought about the officers in all the homes in the city. "All of the British officers aren't like him, I hope."

Elijah shook his head. "No more than all the rebels are dullard troublemakers, I imagine. A few are, of course, but most are like Sam and me. They just want—" He stopped and closed his mouth again. He wasn't used to talking like this—not with me.

I felt Lily's breath on the back of my neck. "Elijah, what can I do?"

"About the mare?" I nodded. "Sam thought about taking her when he left," he said. "But he didn't want to ride at all that late, didn't want to attract attention. There are more British patrols every night."

"Would it be truly safe for her?"

Elijah nodded. "It is a friend's home, I was told. A good and honest man."

"Then I wish Samuel had been able to take Lily," I said quietly.

"I will get word to him."

I caught my breath. "Can you?" He nodded. I glanced toward the door, then turned back. "When?"

"Tomorrow night. Or the one after. I will know soon."

I embraced him quickly, stepping back before either of us had a chance to be embarrassed. "What will you do if there is war, Elijah?"

He shook his head. "I suppose each one has to decide that, each one alone." Elijah stared at his feet for a moment, then met my eyes. "The rebels want to make it so that no king across the ocean decides anything for us over here, so that every man is his own king, most ways. That makes sense to me."

"Thank you, Elijah," I managed, knowing that he had just trusted me with his life. I felt my eyes filling with tears and blinked them back. Then I kissed Lily on the forehead and went back to my chores.

CHAPTER TWELVE

✺ ✺ ✺

*T*hat night, I lay awake again, worrying about my brother. I heard the captain and his aids walk past my door late in the night. They were talking in low voices, but I couldn't understand anything they said. Their boots sounded like thunder on the stairs. I hoped my mother and father could not hear them from their chamber at the other end of the house, that at least someone would sleep this night.

The next morning, at breakfast, Captain Harvey ate without speaking.

"My husband is exhausted with worry and work," my mother told him in a voice both clipped and measured. "He is still abed and needs rest."

I kept my eyes down and didn't utter a single word. The captain ate quickly, then shouted to his men and left. I kept looking out the parlor window until I saw them riding away. Then I went back into the kitchen.

"Prissy, would you kindly begin cleaning up after our guests this morning?" my mother asked. Prissy nodded and smiled as she always did. I had no doubt that the soldiers were dirty and messy and gave her efforts no consideration at all. And if her thoughts ran anything like Elijah's, she must hate them.

"May I help her, Mother?" I asked.

She stared at me. "No, thank you, Silence. I have other work for you."

Prissy shot me a look of gratitude as she left, and I smiled at her. My mother cleared her throat to make me turn back around. We heated water to wash dishes and sand-scrubbed the hearth. Then we carried in kindling from the chopping block where Simon always stacked it. Then, finally, my mother turned to me. "Your father told me something last night I could barely believe," she said quietly. She studied my face. "And you already knew about your brother?"

"I thought it possible," I said carefully.

"Your father seemed even less shocked than you are," she said. "Everyone must have suspected it but me. A traitor to the king. My own son."

She sounded stricken, and I had no idea what to say to her. I stood and tried to embrace her, but she pushed me away very gently. "I just want to know what to believe in," she said quietly, and she sounded, for that instant, like a little girl. Then she stood straighter. "I know that my Samuel has a good heart and that he would never do anything he hadn't thought about long and hard."

"That's absolutely true," I said.

She smiled at me, a tight, bitter smile. "I have been wishing things would change back to the way they were before. Your father has finally convinced me it is impossible."

I nodded. "It seems so."

She took in a sharp breath and looked around the kitchen. "Will you carry the ash bucket to the garden, please?"

Her voice sounded normal, as though nothing was at hand but a day of chores. I tried to match it. "I will, Mother."

Scattering the ashes took less than a moment. I noticed a boy I didn't recognize walking down the lane just past our barn. He was wearing rough workman's clothes. An apprentice at one of the neighbors? Had he been up here to see Elijah?

I set the bucket down and ran across the grass to the barn. Elijah was cleaning hooves. He had

Samuel's gelding tied outside his stall. I rubbed Lily's forehead. "Who was that boy?" I asked quietly.

Elijah shrugged. "A friend." He took a long breath, then whispered. "The meeting is tomorrow night, and Sam intends to come here afterward to get his gelding and Lily."

I thanked him again and glanced up the barn aisle. Simon was watching us. I patted Lily a long time after Elijah went back to work in case Simon thought I had come only to speak to him.

That day passed as slowly as molasses pours in the wintertime. The moments crawled along, seeming to stop altogether now and then. My father finally rose midmorning, and Mother made him breakfast. He sent Prissy on an errand, then asked us both to sit down. "I am sure you have spoken to each other about all this?"

Mother nodded, so I did, too.

He sighed. "After long thought, I have something to tell you both."

I heard my mother take in a breath and hold it.

Father used his napkin, then patted his wig. "My sympathies lie with my son's. The king must let us determine our own fate here. Now," he added before either of us could react, "that doesn't mean I want war. And I still hope we can avoid it. But if we can't, I will not be fighting for the king's right to make decisions for the colonies as though we were a kennel of unruly dogs incapable of speech or discourse."

My mother's eyes flew wide.

I stared at my father, both scared and glad.

"As quickly as we can manage it," he went on, "we will move our household to the countryside, to the farm. Two months ago, I notified by courier the family leasing it, and they replied a week later. It was already their plan to join family in Virginia, and from there to return to England, so they were relieved to be released from the agreement. They have already closed up the house and gone."

"So we will live on the farm?" my mother asked.

My father nodded. "We will take everything we need." He glanced at me. "We will take all the horses with us. The barn there is big enough."

Mother looked almost happy for a moment. If the circumstances had been different, she would have been filled with joy.

"Must we go?" I asked. "What do Sarah's and Anne's fathers plan to do?"

Father shrugged. "I know they are as worried as I am. I will find ways for you to write the girls until things settle. But we must go. The British troops have been digging earthworks." I had no idea what he meant, and I suppose he saw it on my face. "In battles," he said, "big hummocks of dirt are sometimes piled up to protect the soldiers from enemy fire. They are digging in all over the city now. They are preparing for war."

My mother bit her lip. My stomach clenched tight, and my first thought was for my brother. Then I realized I had to fear for my father as well now.

"I wish Samuel would come home," Mother said quietly.

My father touched her cheek, then exhaled. "We all do. I tried to find him, but I could not. I am sure he is hiding somewhere, trying not to bring danger closer to all of us. "

My mother made a little sound of dismay, and he took my hand.

"I've had Elijah and Simon bring packing crates up from the ships at every chance for the past month," Father said. "Today, Simon will fetch a freight wagon, and we'll keep it on the far side of the barn, under the trees, where no one can see it from the house or the lane." He looked at my mother. "Tomorrow, they can both help you fill it with everything that won't be missed by our . . . guests."

I stared at my father. So he had been planning, even before he was sure what he would decide. He *would* keep us safe if he possibly could.

"Are there beds in the farmhouse?" my mother asked. "Wardrobes?"

Father nodded. "Yes, and I have arranged for a drayman to haul whatever furniture you want to take from here." He paused, meeting my eyes. "We must hide our intentions from Captain Harvey and pray that Sam comes back before we leave. I only wish I had some way to get a message to him, to warn him away from here and tell him where we are going."

He continued to look at me. I tried to keep my tangle of emotions from showing on my face. "Captain Harvey has vowed to find and jail your brother if I do not sell him the mare tomorrow—for about a tenth of what she is worth for her bloodlines alone." My father shook his head. "I may have to let her go, Silence, to keep him from hunting Samuel down, and from interfering with our plans."

"But Lily isn't yours," I said without meaning to. "She is mine. You have always said that."

My mother glared at me, then her face softened a little when she saw how near to tears I was. My father looked thoughtful. "I have said that. Over and over. And it might just work. If the mare is not mine, then I can't—"

"But can Silence lawfully own the mare?" my mother asked.

He pursed his lips, thinking. "With me as her guardian, signing the papers, I think she could. It would take a magistrate to say different. I cannot imagine that Captain Harvey will want a day in court, exposed as a bully trying to coerce a young girl. His own men would laugh at that—it'd ruin his reputation as a gentleman, if he has one. If nothing else, it will stall him a few days, and that might be all we need."

I flew into my father's arms, and he held me tightly for an instant, then set me down and went out, calling for Elijah to saddle his horse. I knew it was only a paper, and I knew my father could easily take Lily back, but I was still thrilled at the thought of owning her.

By late afternoon my father had the paper drawn up. He signed as the seller of the mare. I was listed as the buyer. Then he signed again as my guardian, charged with seeing to my welfare and happiness. Anne's and Sarah's fathers had been in town, attending to their own affairs. They had both signed as witnesses.

So, at supper, my father informed Captain Harvey and held up the paper for him to see. The captain laughed a little, then stood. "I have business in town this night," he said, and then left the table without saying another word. We heard him call his aids; a moment later they all left, slamming the front door so hard the sound echoed in the hallway. Their voices rose as they walked toward the pasture. I saw my mother flinch. I ran to the parlor window to hear what they were saying. Captain Harvey was ordering his men to stand watch at the base of the hill. My stomach tightened. I was sure it wasn't to protect us—he hoped to catch Sam.

"I suppose we couldn't expect much different," my father said. He walked to the window and looked out. "He is headed for town. I suspect a night in some tavern is the pressing business involved."

I laid down my napkin. "May I go out to the barn, please?"

"No," my mother said.

But my father held up his hand. "Yes. But not for long."

I thanked him, kissed my mother's cheek to try to ease her heart, then ran to the stables. I told Elijah everything. "Could they be going to look for Samuel?"

"There are several meetings tonight," Elijah said. "But the important one is tomorrow night, and I know he plans to attend. By now he knows that you want him to come get Lily and—"

"Where will that meeting be held?" I interrupted.

He hesitated, then a look of understanding came into his eyes. "Past Faneuil Market, down toward the docks. It's a shipper's warehouse." He shrugged. "Empty, of course, with nothing coming ashore for so long. Paul Revere, John Hancock, Sam Adams—all the leaders will be there. They hope to reach a final agreement about what course to take."

I knew what I had to do; I was just afraid to do it. For an instant I thought about asking Elijah to help me, but I couldn't. He was an indentured servant, and if a patrol of British soldiers caught him in the dark of the night with a horse, they would assume he was a thief.

"When?" I whispered.

Elijah look into my eyes for a long moment. "Midnight," he said.

"Will you saddle Lily and Sam's gelding for me at eleven tomorrow night?"

He nodded.

I thanked him, then turned and walked back to the house, wondering if I should tell either of my parents. By the time I opened the door, I knew I couldn't. They would stop me because they loved me and wanted me safe. But I had to go. For Lily, for myself, and to warn Samuel.

CHAPTER THIRTEEN

❧ ❧ ❧

*M*y mother, Prissy, and I spent the morn ing—once Captain Harvey and his men had ridden off—packing up almost everything. Clothing, my parent's formal wigs, keepsakes of all kinds, my mother's quilts and tapestries, boxes of candles, spare lanterns and oil lamps, her kitchen scales and crockery from the pantry, washbasins, bed linens, everything you can think of and more. For several hours, my father helped Elijah and Simon carry the full crates out to the freight wagon. Then he saddled a horse and rode into the city to attend to what he called "other matters." I hoped that meant he would try again to find Sam.

"I am afraid," Prissy said when my mother left the room to tend the stew we would be eating for dinner.

I looked up from the crate that held my mother's creamware washbasins and nodded. "I am, too."

Prissy looked deep into my eyes. "If anything happens to your father, do you think Mr. Samuel would keep the promise to free me when I turn thirty?"

The question startled me, then made me feel terribly selfish. I had not once considered that Prissy would be concerned about my father's safety for her own reasons. "Sam would probably do it sooner," I told her. "And if it were somehow up to me, it would be tomorrow." I hadn't known I was going to say it, but the tears that flooded into her eyes made me very glad I had. I meant it. A fair and kind master was still a master. If freedom was right for the colonies, for the rest of us, it had to be right for slaves, too.

Prissy dabbed at her eyes and made a shooing motion. "Keep working. Your mother will soon be back. Let's not upset her today of all days." I nodded. And with all of us working hard, we had half the household loaded onto the wagon before noon. By the time Captain Harvey arrived, we were all in the kitchen, busy at our usual chores, and Father had come back.

The captain ate stew with relish, then lay down his spoon. "I think I saw your son last night," he said quietly.

Father looked up sharply, then shrugged and lied. "I doubt that. He slept soundly here. I sent him off early to see to some business for me."

I held my breath. Captain Harvey just smiled thinly and went back to eating.

I had to fight my inclination to stare at him. I had come to hate him. But I was afraid that any expression of my anger would alert him, make him hunt harder for Samuel, trump up some reason to arrest him—or my father.

I ate, tasting nothing, barely able to stay in my chair, and I tried to comfort myself with the thought that we were about to disappear for good, going where Captain Harvey could not bully my father into doing anything. One more night was all we needed. I would warn Samuel not to come to the house at all, just to leave Boston with Lily and meet us at the country house in a few days.

I saw Captain Harvey glance up at the hearth, and my pulse quickened. But nothing looked different in the kitchen, we had been very careful of that. It was only our bedchambers that were nearly empty—and the pantry that had held the cast-iron

"If I *were* a boy—" I began.

Sam shook his head, grinning. "If you were a boy, I would have to pity the king. Give our parents my love." He stepped back, and the moonlight lit his face.

I smiled, then looked past him and saw a man riding toward us. Most were on foot, so he stood out—and he looked oddly familiar. It took a moment for me to recognize him without his uniform.

"Sam, look," I whispered. "On the bay horse. That's Captain Harvey."

"Stay here," he whispered back.

And before I could argue with him, Samuel went inside the building. A moment later he came out, and there were fifteen or twenty men with him.

"Stop there, sir." One of them called out. "Are you Captain Harvey?"

I watched the captain rein in, startled.

"You are on private property, sir," the man shouted. Captain Harvey looked angry, but he said nothing.

Samuel came to stand beside me. "I only hope he doesn't go for help."

I leaned down. "Shout an insult at him, Samuel. Loud. Use his name and make it a good one."

I backed the gelding up a step or two while Samuel stared at me. "Why?"

I tested the cinch, then settled myself in the saddle. "So he thinks that I am you when I gallop off. I'll lead him away from here, away from you and from Lily—and everyone else."

"Silence, you can't—"

"You know I *can,*" I cut him off. "Insult him. Make it something he can't ignore without getting laughed at. Then step back into the shadows." I tucked my ponytail down the back of Elijah's shirt. Sam's hair wasn't as long as mine.

There was a long pause, then Samuel took the bridle and led his horse forward a half step—so that he stood next to the gelding's head in the moonlight and I was still deep in the shadows.

Then he lifted his head and shouted. "Captain Harvey! Where's your uniform? Did you decide that red doesn't flatter you?"

That made the men laugh, but Sam wasn't finished. "This man has been trying to steal my sister's mare," he called out. "But I don't think he could handle such a spirited horse." There were jeers and whistles from the shadows beneath the trees. "My little sister is twice the man he'll ever be," Sam yelled, and the growing crowd burst into laughter.

back past him, urging Sam's gelding faster, flying along our usual course until we were racing toward the edge of the marsh. I held my breath.

It worked perfectly.

Sam's gelding knew exactly where the tree stump was in the moonlight; as far as he was concerned, this was just another race—and he was winning this time. I held him straight as long as I dared, then reined in, just a little. Captain Harvey was so intent on catching me on what looked like a straightaway that he whipped his horse onward, straight into the shallow marsh water, as I leaned into the turn I knew was coming. I heard the captain cursing as Samuel's gelding rounded the sharp turn neatly and pounded away, headed back for the lane of maple trees as always. When we got there, I pulled him back to a walk, then stopped so I could hear.

Captain Harvey wasn't shouting now. His voice had a low, wheedling tone. I heard hoofbeats in the darkness, a trotting cadence that slowed after a moment. Then Captain Harvey cursed again. I could not help but smile. He had been thrown off, and the horse had gotten away from him. Perfect. Captain Harvey would be busy for quite some time.

I cantered back over the Common, making sure he could hear me going back toward the meeting. Then, once I was sure he could no longer hear the gelding's hoofbeats, I reined in and rode a different route home, keeping the gelding to a walk. I listened intently, and I rode back the way I had left, stopping once to let another patrol pass us by in the darkness.

My father was waiting for me in the barn. I caught my breath, then lifted my head, ready to stand any punishment he thought I deserved for worrying him like this. Then I saw Elijah standing by him. Their faces were anxious, lit by the lantern my father held high. He didn't scold me, and he didn't look angry. He had only two questions.

"Are you all right?"

And once I nodded, he let out a long breath, then asked this: "And Samuel? Did you find him? Elijah will not tell me and break his word, but I cannot imagine any other reason for your doing this."

I dismounted and saw his eyebrows shoot upward when he noticed my attire and the man's saddle on the gelding. I started explaining. I told my father everything. His face was furrowed with worry and anger when I began. By the end of the story, he looked as though he was trying not to smile.

"Go to bed, daughter," he said. "We have an exceedingly full day on the morrow."

I bade them both good night, fetched my dress from the bushes, and went inside. Lying in bed, I found myself feeling absurdly happy. We weren't done yet, and Captain Harvey was going to be angry. But Lily was safe, as was Sam, and that was enough for one night.

CHAPTER FOURTEEN

❧ ❧ ❧

*M*orning came quickly. I rose and went into the kitchen to find Captain Harvey sitting at the table. He did not speak to me at all, nor to my mother. He simply ate, shoved his charger away as he stood—then left with his men. I peeked out the window. He had caught his horse. They saddled up and rode at a canter down the lane. Wherever he was going, he was in a hurry.

The instant he was gone, my mother ran down the hall. I heard banging and thudding a moment later, and went to see. There were four men with my father in my parents' bedchamber. The draymen had arrived before first light and hidden their wagon in the trees beside the barn. They had been waiting quietly since for Captain Harvey and his men to be gone.

My father explained that we were taking only the furniture that had been gifted to my parents when they married—everything else would stay. My mother was packing foodstuffs, too, the meat and cheeses from the smokehouse and pantry, and all she could gather from her garden.

So before noon, we were riding south—my mother and Prissy settled in the wagon, Elijah, my father, and me riding alongside. I could only suppose that when Captain Harvey and his men came home expecting to be served a midday dinner, they would be surprised to find a cold hearth, an empty house, an empty barn, not a bite of food in the pantry, and a garden that had been harvested early.

It took us three long days to get to the farm. We slept in fields, using my mother's oldest blankets. When we arrived, every one of us travel sore and tired, Simon greeted us with a hearth fire and a kettle of tea. I saw my father's face tighten a little, and my own heart fell, when Simon told us he had not seen Samuel yet.

Mother put us to work almost immediately. The house really was quite clean, so my first chore was carrying in firewood. It was wonderfully quiet, and there was a rocky little creek that ran through the place—I could hear it from my new bedchamber. The barn was down a slope from the house—and my window had shutters. That made me smile.

I looked up the road a hundred times that day, wishing, hoping to see my lovely cream-colored mare cantering toward me, my brother safe and sound on her back. But they did not come.

It was hard to fall asleep in a strange place, but I was weary and finally did. And with the sunrise came the most beautiful sound of all. Hoofbeats. I leaped from bed and dragged my clothes on, nearly tearing my stockings when they tangled.

Samuel whooped when he saw me, and we had a long moment of his swinging me off my feet into a circle—the kind of hug I had loved when I was little. Then we just clung to each other for a moment more, stepping back when we heard Father shout Sam's name. Mother came out of the house at a run. Sam handed me Lily's reins and went to meet them.

Lily nuzzled me. The familiar tickle of her breath on my skin made me smile even as my eyes glossed over with tears of relief. There. We were all here now. I knew Sam would not hide when the war came. Nor would my father. And I knew that independence from England and the king would not be easily won. But at that moment, I had no doubt it would be achieved.

The colonies were full of independent people. Sam was right. There was something different about us—everyone I knew looked toward the future and wanted to shape their own lives. I certainly did. Maybe Elijah and my brother would want a third partner in their horse farm. They both knew I would do my share of the work. I was sure Simon would want to stay with my mother. But maybe we could all go visit Prissy and her family one day once she was free. And I would write to Anne and Sarah both, so we didn't lose touch and . . .

Lily nuzzled me again, nudging me gently on my shoulder—she was both tired and hungry. I led her toward the barn, the rein slack between us, her muzzle almost resting on my shoulder as we went down the hill.